Johnny s
on the s

her shoulder.

"Relax," he whispered close to her ear. "I'm doing you a favor."

Jenn's mind scrambled for an answer to his riddle, but to save her life she couldn't put two thoughts together rationally as her family returned to the room.

"Thanks, folks," Johnny said, addressing them. "It was nice to have a few minutes alone with Jenn to get reacquainted with this lovely lady."

His arm tightened around her shoulder for just a moment. She didn't know if the gesture was meant for the family's benefit or if he was sending her some kind of unspoken message.

Maybe both.

Because she was sure, now, what he was doing.

He was playing her game.

Books by Deb Kastner

Love Inspired

A Holiday Prayer
Daddy's Home
Black Hills Bride
The Forgiving Heart
A Daddy at Heart
A Perfect Match
The Christmas Groom
Hart's Harbor
Undercover Blessings
The Heart of a Man
A Wedding in Wyoming

DEB KASTNER

lives and writes in colorful Colorado with the Front Range of the Rocky Mountains for inspiration. She loves writing for the Steeple Hill Love Inspired line, where she can write about her two favorite things—faith and love. Her characters range from upbeat and humorous to (her favorite) dark and brooding heroes. Her plots fall anywhere between, from a playful romp to the deeply emotional.

Two of Deb's books have been nominated for an *RT Book Reviews* Reviewer's Award for Best Book of the Year for Steeple Hill.

Deb and her husband share their home with their two youngest daughters. Deb is thrilled about the newest member of the family—her first granddaughter, Isabella. What fun to be a granny!

Deb loves to hear from her readers. You can contact her by e-mail at DEBWRTR@aol.com, or on her MySpace or Facebook pages.

A Wedding in Wyoming
Deb Kastner

Steeple
Hill®

Published by Steeple Hill Books™

STEEPLE HILL BOOKS

Steeple
Hill®

Recycling programs
for this product may
not exist in your area.

ISBN-13: 978-0-373-87570-2

A WEDDING IN WYOMING

Copyright © 2009 by Debra Kastner

Printed in U.S.A.

But he was wounded for our transgressions,
He was bruised for our iniquities:
The chastisement for our peace was upon Him,
And by His stripes we are healed.
                              —*Isaiah* 53:5

To my former manager Kristie Parks at Hallmark, and all the ladies, for making my time working there so special. I told you I would!

To my editor, Emily Rodmell, for her patience and direction in bringing me back up to speed in my career with this book.

And most of all, to my family—my husband, Joe, my daughter Annie and her husband, Max, and my daughters Kimberly and Katie. You have pulled with me through the rough times and laughed with me through our joy. May God continue to bless each and every one of you with His mercy, grace and love.

Much excitement and love to the little new bobbit in the DePriest/Kastner family, my first granddaughter, Isabella! And no—I'm *not* old enough to be a Granny!

Chapter One

The roses were perfect, and so was her plan.

This year, Jenn Washington's annual two-week family reunion would be different. She could see it already, from the way her family was fawning over the recently delivered bouquet.

"Oh, how lovely!" Jenn's mother exclaimed. "And to be delivered way out here—it's such a romantic gesture."

"A dozen red roses," Granny added, waggling her eyebrows suggestively. "The color of love."

Precisely, thought Jenn. *Thank you very much.*

She'd gone to a great deal of trouble picking out the perfect bouquet online—red roses surrounded by a scattering of baby's breath and lodged in a lovely French vase. It had cost her a pretty penny, not only to purchase, but to have them sent by special courier to the middle of nowhere in Wyoming, at her grandparent's ranch where she'd grown up.

Now, seeing her family's surprised gazes, she knew it was worth every cent.

This plan was going to work.

"Sounds fishy to me," Jenn's great-aunt, Myra, said, pursing her lips. "There's a card attached. Let's read it."

"Don't you think you ought to let Jenn read it in private? It's her gift, after all," Granddad said in his usual, pleasantly gruff manner.

All eyes were on Jenn. Her heart was pounding. This was the moment she'd waited for, her coup de grace, so to speak. "Oh, no, that's all right. Go ahead and read it. I have no secrets."

She had more secrets than she cared to admit, but she wouldn't reveal a single one.

Not now.

Not ever.

Auntie Myra plucked up the small card and opened it with flair, clearing her throat melodramatically before reading the words.

"'Love, Me.'"

Clever, even if Jenn had to say so herself. She wanted to laugh aloud, but she kept her expression as innocently neutral as she was able.

"That's it?" Granny said, turning to face Jenn, arms akimbo. "Sounds like you've got a bit of explaining to do, missy."

Jenn did her best to look both innocent and delighted. *Delighted* wasn't so difficult. This was going to be fun. No one was going to tease her about a lack of a significant other this year. No one was going to hint at the lack of grandchildren at the reunion.

Not this year.

Exactly as she'd planned.

"They're just flowers," she said, making a dismissive

motion with her hand. "I don't know why everyone is making such a big deal over it."

"What? You don't like flowers now?" teased Granny.

"Oh, I like flowers," Jenn answered with a laugh.

"So it's the *man* you don't like," guessed Jenn's mother.

Jenn laughed again and shook her head. "I didn't say that."

"Do you even know who these are from?" queried Auntie Myra, still gazing at Jenn with suspicion and disbelief. Not hard to understand, since Jenn, now twenty-six, had never brought a man home to meet the family.

"Of course I do," Jenn answered immediately.

Me, she thought with delight.

"And that would be?" Auntie Myra continued.

From the start, she'd known that her family would want to know the name, rank and serial number of any man who'd *finally* gotten close enough to Jenn to receive her attention.

"J-uh-Johnny," she stammered, and then let out a relieved breath when everyone smiled at her.

All at once, questions flew at her from every direction.

Where did she meet him?

How long had they been dating?

Why hadn't she mentioned him before?

As quick as they started, the barrage of questions were abruptly cut off by a loud pounding coming from behind them.

"What's all the noise in here?" came an unexpected voice from the kitchen doorway, where a sandy-haired man was lounging his bony shoulder against the doorway, his cowboy hat low over his eyes.

"Scotty!" Jenn was the first to see him, and launched

herself into his arms, nearly knocking him off his feet. "I didn't think you were coming!"

"Young man," Granny said, from just over Jenn's shoulder, "didn't your mama teach you any manners? A gentleman removes his hat when he enters a house."

Scotty colored and swept off the dusty blue cavalry hat, his trademark among the bull riders from back in his teen years, tapping it mildly against his thigh. He cleared his throat loudly. "Sorry, Granny."

Granny made an indistinct snorting sound, then laughed, crowding Jenn to give her grandson a hug. It wasn't a moment more before everyone was crowding in for a big family bear hug.

Scotty was a welcome diversion from Jenn's flowers, a fact she noticed and was happy to accommodate. She'd rather not answer the questions her family plagued her with about her mysterious Johnny, so it was just as well.

And she was as thrilled as the rest of her family to see her baby brother. It had been a year, and he had sprouted like a beanpole.

It was only then, stepping back to allow her family more access to her brother, that she noticed Scotty was not alone. Lingering in the background behind her brother, his hip leaned negligently against the kitchen counter, his black Diamond Jim Stetson curled in his hand, was another man, a stranger to Jenn.

He was tall, six two maybe, with broad shoulders and strong arms, but with the long, wiry frame of a man who spent most of his time in the saddle. His deep, curly black hair was a little long, as if he'd missed his last haircut, and was ruffled from the removal from his hat. He was purposefully hanging back, but his posture was relaxed and his face friendly and open. Jenn guessed the cowboy could be called handsome, in a rugged sort of way.

If one were attracted to that sort of man, which Jenn definitely wasn't.

He'd obviously come in with her brother, though he looked to be several years older than Scotty—close to Jenn's own age, she guessed.

He didn't look uncomfortable at being overlooked. His dark eyes, a color which floated somewhere between blue and black, were brimming with amusement and understanding. His friend was home with family, who clearly adored him. The stranger appeared to be content to wait his turn.

When the man realized Jenn was staring at him, he smiled and winked at her. Flushing, she turned her gaze away and elbowed Auntie Myra, gesturing toward the unannounced guest, knowing her aunt would jump at the chance to welcome someone new to their gathering, especially a handsome young man.

"Why, Scotty," Auntie Myra exclaimed, "you haven't introduced your guest."

Scotty laughed from his belly and gestured the stranger forward, slapping him on the back affectionately. "Sorry. I was so caught up in seeing you all I almost forgot about him."

"Well, thanks," the stranger replied, punching Scotty's arm hard enough to send the boy off balance and sprawling into other family members.

"I can introduce myself," the man said, his voice deep, yet surprisingly soft-spoken, given his size. He had the slightest bit of a drawl, though not Texan nor Southern. Jenn couldn't place it.

She was pondering this when his next words blasted over her with the force of a hurricane.

"Glad to meet ya'll. My name's Johnny. Johnny Barnes."

Dead silence.

Even loquacious Auntie Myra was left speechless in the wake of Johnny's declaration.

Jenn's breath left her body as if she'd been punched in the gut. And it didn't return. She wasn't even sure her heart was beating.

Johnny?

Scotty brings a wrangler from the depths of Wyoming and his name is *Johnny?*

It figured. It just figured. Now she was going to have to talk her way out of this one, too, because she knew perfectly well her dear family was never going to leave it alone.

So, what if there were a million *Johnnys* in the world? They were still going to ask if he was the *one,* Jenn just knew it. And the expressions on her family's faces only served to confirm her fears. Especially Auntie Myra, who looked as if she was preparing to pounce on the poor cowboy.

Scotty looked around, obviously confused by his family's odd behavior. Everyone else's gaze was on Jenn. No one was welcoming Scotty's new friend to the household, as her younger brother had clearly expected.

"Johnny wrangles with me. I thought it would be okay to bring him along," Scotty said, hesitantly.

Granddad was the first to recover, always the most sensible of the lot of them. "Of course he's welcome.

Johnny, glad to meet you." Granddad thrust out his hand for a hearty handshake.

Auntie Myra stepped forward and hugged the man. Johnny returned the unexpected embrace awkwardly, and Jenn smiled despite herself. Obviously, Johnny was not prepared for Scotty's affectionate family, as he accepted hug after hug from the women and friendly, enthusiastic handshakes from the men.

Only Jenn remained where she was, caught in a trap of her own making. She couldn't approach the man and greet him. Stranger or friend, her family would be watching her with hawkeyes.

It took a moment, but her brain slowly started functioning again.

What did she have to worry about? This was Scotty's friend, fresh from sprawling Wyoming ranch land. Surely her family would realize he couldn't possibly be *her* Johnny.

There would only be a moment of confusion before things were set to right and she could go back to enjoying the reunion.

"So," asked Auntie Myra in a casual tone that belied her open, wide-eyed curiosity, "Are you *the* Johnny we've heard about?"

Jenn cringed inwardly, though she reminded herself again and again there was no real danger in him answering that question. The man wouldn't have the slightest notion of what Auntie Myra was really asking, and would, naturally, answer to the negative.

End of subject.

Johnny definitely looked stunned as he stared from face to face. But after a moment he quirked his lips, shrugged, and announced, "Guess I've been found out. Yes, ma'am. That would be me."

Jenn felt her legs buckle underneath her and moved quickly to the sofa and sat before she fell down. She had no idea why the unknown cowboy had answered the way he had, but now she—and he, for that matter—had, as the old saying went, a lot of 'splaining to do.

She was suddenly furious at the gall of the cowboy. Never mind that this whole set up was her doing in the first place.

How could he say he was *the* Johnny? There was *no* Johnny! What kind of a game was he playing?

Everyone rushed at him at once, deluging him with questions.

When had he met Jenn?

How long had they been together?

And how long had it been since they'd seen each other last, what with him wrangling and all?

Johnny sent a panicked glance at Scotty, but his friend just grinned and shrugged. Obviously the boy would be no help in sorting this out.

Who was *Jenn?* What were these nutty people talking about?

Suddenly he spied the young woman seated on the sofa, the pretty woman who'd been the first to notice him when he and Scotty first arrived. She was also, he'd noted, the only one of her spirited family who'd held back in the initial greeting, not offering him a welcome, much less a hug. She must be the sister Scotty had mentioned.

She now looked a little woozy. Her eyes looked

glazed over and she was gripping the arm of the sofa like a lifeline. He guessed her to be around his age—twenty-five or twenty-six at most. She had gorgeous, short golden curls, a pretty, perky little nose, intelligent blue eyes, and a face as red as a Macintosh apple.

Obviously, she was the woman they were all talking about. What he didn't know was *what* they were talking about.

He'd thought Scotty's family had recognized him from a magazine cover or a television news story, but apparently that was not the case. He didn't know whether to be relieved or alarmed.

He had to figure out what was going on, and fast. He thrust his fingers through his hair and tapped his Stetson against his thigh. If these people didn't know who he really was—and they clearly didn't—he didn't want to tip off his own hand.

He hesitated in revealing his true identity—just yet. Not to this happy, *real* family who apparently didn't keep up with national news all that well.

But he still didn't know who they thought he was. He had to figure out some way to gain the information he needed without giving himself away.

And then he realized the answer to his problem, that *other way,* was staring straight back at him, half glaring, half beckoning, as if she expected him to say something that would clear up everything. To say that he was in no way connected with her, apparently.

And he supposed he would…in time. At the moment, he just wanted to hear what was invariably going to be a highly amusing story, especially if it came from the mouth of the lovely woman on the sofa.

He grinned widely as he looked away from Jenn and tipped his head toward her aunt, his fingers tugging at the imaginary brim of his hat. *Cowboy style,* he thought, his smile growing even bigger. "I'm mighty pleased to meet you all," he said, giving a show at his most charming drawl. "But I wonder if I might have a moment alone with—uh,—Jenn?"

He couldn't remember everyone's names in the enthusiastic jumble of introductions, but Jenn's name was sealed firmly in his mind.

"Why, of course," answered a fine-looking middle-age woman who could only be Scotty and Jenn's mother. She had the same golden curls—albeit with a bit of white—and the same vibrant blue eyes as her daughter. "You two probably haven't seen each other in ages."

Which was the understatement of the century, Johnny thought, his lips twitching with amusement.

"We'll all retire to the kitchen to get sandwiches prepared for everyone," Jenn's grandmother suggested, "and give you two a little privacy."

Jenn was on her feet in an instant. "I don't think—" She stopped, looking around with wide eyes. *A deer caught in the headlights,* Johnny thought. She looked as if she were about to be run over by a blaring semi truck.

Johnny still had absolutely no idea what was going on, but it had to be one good story. He probably would have laughed out loud if the poor young woman by the sofa didn't look so pitifully miserable.

He hadn't felt like laughing—really laughing—in a very long time, and he savored the feeling. He'd let his work get the best of him, stealing away his teenage years, not to mention the first half of his twenties. Taking this summer off was the best thing that had ever happened to him.

Especially now, when he'd somehow landed in the midst of a happy, if chaotic, family, and a mystery he was eager to solve.

"Now, Jenn," said Scotty's and Jenn's grandmother, "be gracious to your guest. Fresh-ground coffee is on its way." She turned to Johnny. "Please, young man, be seated." Her forceful sideways glance at Jenn clearly indicated she should do the same.

Jenn nodded mutely at her family as all but her brother departed for the kitchen.

Scotty didn't budge. He was grinning at Johnny like he'd just roped a steer on the first try. Scotty didn't speak, but he chuckled and lifted one eyebrow.

Johnny just shrugged.

"Scotty," Jenn said, her voice just a little bit shaky and very much pleading, "please."

Scotty laughed rowdily but moved to join the others in the kitchen.

Jenn cringed inwardly. Count on her baby brother to give her trouble about this. About *Johnny*. As if she weren't in enough trouble already.

Jenn regained her seat on the sofa with a deep sigh, burying her face in her hands. Johnny sat down on an armchair opposite her, leaned his elbows on his legs, and waited.

Jenn said nothing for the longest time. This was absolutely, totally surreal. She couldn't get her mind around what was happening, never mind what to do with the situation.

She was alone in a room with a man she'd just now met—a man whom her family assumed was some sort of *significant other* in her life, a relationship obviously serious enough to warrant flowers being delivered to her out in the middle of nowhere.

Quickly, she composed her thoughts. There had to be a simple way out of this mess, even if she couldn't see it now. She just had to think rationally. Starting with the obvious.

"Why did you call yourself *the* Johnny?" she asked, her voice more demanding than she'd intended, but she was under a lot of strain.

"We'll get to that," the man replied in his soft, rich baritone. "But first, I think you need to tell me who these people think I am."

Jenn nodded. "Yes, I suppose you're right. You must be stupefied by their reaction to your presence."

He laughed. "Yeah, well, *stupefied* isn't the exact word I'd use, but let's just say I am more than just curious."

She couldn't help but laugh with him. It *was* funny, or at least it would be in twenty years when she looked back on this moment.

Right this second though, she felt dreadfully serious. Her stomach hurt.

"It's my family. I know you've only just met them, but I'm sure you've noticed how overwhelming they can be."

"You're lucky to have a family," Johnny said, his expression suddenly serious. Then he smiled and shrugged. "I'm an orphan, myself."

"Oh, I'm sorry," she said, and meant it with all her heart. Her job as a social worker in downtown Denver brought her in contact with many orphaned and abandoned children. She knew firsthand the pain and suffering they experienced, being all alone in the world. She wondered what Johnny's story was, what he had been through. But now was not the time to ask.

"I love my family, I really do," she stated emphatically. "I look forward to these yearly gatherings. It's the only time I see most of my family, even my parents. I work in Denver, and it sometimes feels like Wyoming—where the rest of my family lives—might as well be Mars."

"You're busy with your work?" Johnny asked.

He had guessed accurately. "Yes. I'm a social worker. I work long, hard hours—sometimes seven days a week. And I'm on call many of the nights."

Johnny nodded. "I know what you mean."

She supposed he did, in a backward, cowboy sort of way. Wrangling cattle was pretty much a 24/7 job.

"There's just this one thing, you see," she explained. Oddly, she was beginning to feel comfortable in this cowboy's presence. He was a large, intimidating man, to be sure, but he had kind eyes and a playful quirk to his lips that set her at ease.

Still, she had to be careful where she trod, especially since Johnny seemed so sincere.

It was best simply to get down to business and have it done with. They needed to work out a feasible solution to the problem she'd created, not become friends. Not that she wanted that, anyway.

"You may have noticed there are no children about."

He cocked his head a little to one side, and then nodded. "I have to admit I was a little surprised—a family reunion with no kids."

"My Auntie Myra—she's my great-aunt, really—lost her husband in Vietnam. They had no children, and her heart was so broken she never remarried."

"I see," he said, though the look on his face told her he had no idea whatsoever where this conversation was leading.

"Basically, Johnny, the lot has fallen on me. Everyone wants squealing little children running rampant through this farm, and they want them now."

"Well, sure they do," he said with a soft drawl. "But you're all of what, twenty-four years old? Twenty-five, maybe? And Scotty's only just finished his high school diploma."

"I'm twenty-six," Jenn clarified wryly. "And as far as my family is concerned, it's time for me to settle down and start popping out some sweet little babies for them to spoil rotten."

She paused thoughtfully. "It's not all that surprising, really, given everyone's circumstances. I don't blame them. It's just not where I'm at in my life right now."

Ever, she thought grimly, but she didn't say the word aloud.

Johnny pursed his lips. "So, then, let's see. The real problem is that Mr. Right hasn't come along yet to sweep you off your feet?"

Jenn chuckled. "I don't even know if there is such a man. For me, at least."

"You're pulling my leg," he replied, with a shake of his head. "You can't tell me you don't have men knocking down your door every day of the week. A beautiful, intelligent woman like you?"

He was teasing, but that didn't stop Jenn from flushing from her toes to the tips of her ears. "I really don't have time for dating."

"Well, you ought to make some." His midnight-blue eyes were alight with amusement.

Jenn waved him off with her hand. "Now you're starting to sound like my family."

He laughed and stretched like a lazy cat. He was so large he dwarfed the armchair he was seated on.

"I still don't understand where I come in," he said after a minute.

"You don't," she stated emphatically. "This is all one big misunderstanding."

"I got that much. So who is—and more to the point *where* is—this fellow Johnny your family was clearly expecting?"

She groaned and put a palm to her forehead. "That's the thing," she muttered. "There is no Johnny."

There was another long moment's pause as Johnny considered her words, and then he shook his head. "I don't get it."

She chuckled. "No, you wouldn't. I did something stupid, at least in hindsight it appears that way. My family always teases me mercilessly about getting married and starting a family, so I made up a man."

"You did *what?*" He fingered the dusty Stetson in his hand.

"It's not as complicated as it sounds—at least it *wasn't,* until you showed up and announced your name was Johnny."

"My name *is* Johnny," he said with a low chuckle.

"Unfortunately," she muttered, and then clapped a

hand over her mouth. "I'm so sorry. I really didn't mean that the way it sounded."

He laughed. "I didn't think you did."

She liked his laugh. He threw back his head and chortled wholeheartedly, his blue eyes glittering.

Okay, so she was harboring a little resentment toward the man, even if she knew perfectly well it wasn't really his fault she was in this predicament. Fortunately, he couldn't tell how she was really feeling, this convulsion of emotions coursing through her heart and head.

At least Johnny appeared to be taking her revelations with courtesy and maybe a touch of humor, which, Jenn thought, said a lot about the kind of man he was. He didn't seem mad at her.

Yet.

He hadn't heard the whole story. Johnny might appear to be a nice enough man for an unpolished cowboy, but he still had no idea how big a quandary he'd innocently walked into.

There were limits to any man's patience, and Johnny's, she had to think, must already be stretched close to its limit.

Jenn was about to continue her convoluted explanation when her mother interrupted. Clearing her throat loudly to announce her presence, Jenn's mother entered with two steaming mugs of freshly ground and brewed coffee. Jenn inhaled the lovely aroma of hazelnut and crème, her favorite.

Mom didn't say a word. She set the mugs on the table and, with an encouraging smile to each of them, backtracked into the kitchen, closing the French doors that separated the rooms firmly behind her.

"I sent myself flowers," Jenn announced as soon as she and Johnny were once more alone.

"That's it?" Johnny asked, cocking an eyebrow. "That's all you did? Signed the card *Johnny* and let everyone think what they may?"

"Not exactly," she said, chuckling. "I signed the card, *Love, Me.*"

He laughed heartily, and Jenn was certain her family could hear *that* from the next room.

"Clever," he said. "Ingenious. This story gets better and better. So what happened when the flowers arrived?" He leaned forward, elbows on his knees, as if anxious to hear the rest.

In that, he would be disappointed. "There isn't much to tell. The family made a big deal of it, of course, and started nagging me for a name. I'd only just blurted out *Johnny* when you and Scotty showed up."

"Hmm," he said, stroking his strong jaw between his thumb and forefinger. His face was unshaven, as he'd been out on the range for a good week at least, Jenn thought.

She wondered why she didn't find the scruff unattractive. Stubble had never appealed to her before.

He sat back in the chair. "My showing up puts you in a bit of a pickle, doesn't it?"

"Let's just say it was a major jolt to my system, and leave it at that. I was really freaked out there for a while. But now that I've had a chance to settle down and think about it—and to talk to you—it's really not so bad. We—*I*, that is,—just need to come clean with the facts. I simply have to tell my family there's been a misunderstanding and you are not *my* Johnny."

"And yet, here we've been sitting alone all this time like we're catching up."

The man did have a point. Jenn felt herself blushing again. She hated that. "I can't think of how to explain that part—yet."

Johnny grinned. "I can."

But before he could say more, the family emerged from the kitchen, flooding back into the living room with expectant gazes on their faces. Apparently, they'd collectively decided they'd waited long enough to get the scoop on Jenn and her new beau.

Even Scotty looked curious. *How could he think for one second that...*

Her thoughts were cut off when Johnny stood, and with the athletic agility of a rugged cowboy, slid into the spot next to her on the sofa and slipped his arm around her shoulders, effectively sealing the deal.

She couldn't think. She couldn't breathe. The temperature in the room seemed to suddenly have spiked to well over two hundred degrees.

What was the crazy cowboy up to now? Didn't he realize he was making things worse by the second?

And how was she going to explain herself to her family, when Johnny was acting so cozy with her?

There was only one answer to that question.

She couldn't.

Chapter Two

"Relax," he whispered close to her ear, his soft drawl sending a shiver down her spine for any number of reasons. "I'm doing you a favor."

What? Her mind scrambled for an answer to his riddle, but she couldn't put two thoughts together rationally to save her life.

Steady, she coaxed herself mentally. *Relax. Think. Try to locate your brain.*

"Thanks, folks," Johnny said, addressing her hovering family. "It was nice to have a few minutes alone with Jenn to get—er—*reacquainted* with this lovely lady."

His arm tightened around her shoulder for just a moment. She didn't know if the gesture was meant for the family's benefit or if he was sending her some kind of unspoken message.

Maybe both.

Because she was sure, now, what he was doing.

He was playing her game.

The game *she* had initiated and no longer wanted any part of.

She tried to speak, to lay it all on the line for her family, but Johnny's statement sent the whole clan abuzz, and Jenn couldn't get a word in edgewise.

"A *cowboy*," Granny said, looking from Johnny to Jenn, and then back at Johnny again, assessing them before giving Jenn a nod of approval. "Who would have thought?"

Who would have thought, indeed? Jenn wouldn't hog-tie herself to a ranch hand in a million years. Rough-and-tumble cowboys just weren't her type, and her family, of all people, should have known that.

"The flowers are lovely," her mother offered.

Especially picked for me, by me, Jenn thought.

"And how romantic for you two to meet up this way," Auntie Myra added. "Johnny must have done some real fast talking to surprise you like this, Jenn. All in all, I think this whole reunion is going to be one surprise after another."

More than Auntie Myra could possibly know.

Granddad settled into the chocolate-colored armchair Johnny had vacated. "So, son, tell us more about you. Jenn was going to fill us in when you arrived. Where do you hail from?"

Jenn noticed Johnny's hesitation, and the way his grip on his cowboy hat tightened. He rolled the rim as he spoke. "I'm originally from Nebraska, sir, but I've lived all over the country at one time or another."

That explained the slight but unidentifiable drawl, at any rate—the accent that made her heart do that tiny, annoying flutter she was trying to ignore. Johnny spoke firmly and quietly, but the tension was definitely still present.

Jenn wondered if anyone else had noticed the way he'd suddenly stiffened. But no, of course not—they were all flying off in this wild fantasy she had created for their benefit. She wanted to crawl underneath the nearest chair and hide, but Johnny's arm was still firmly about her shoulders.

"Your family is in Nebraska?" Jenn's father asked, standing directly behind the armchair her grandfather occupied and leaning into it, resting his elbow on the cushion.

"No family," Johnny said briskly. He wanted to fold his arms across his chest in a protective move, but he didn't want to let go of Jenn to do it, so he remained where he was. He didn't want to talk about this subject—not to this nice, close, happy family. But he knew he had to say something. "I'm an orphan, sir."

Best to stay as close to the truth as possible, he decided. As a Christian, it went against every moral grain in his body to submit even the smallest white lie to anyone, but he'd suddenly discovered a chivalrous streak he hadn't even known he possessed until this moment.

At first, this charade had been about himself, about protecting his own identity and getting to spend a couple weeks finding out how a real family functioned.

Now it was about Jenn.

When the family had abruptly broken off his conversation with Jenn, he'd moved to her side without a moment's thought or hesitation, going straight on gut instinct. An instinct to protect the beautiful woman now lodged firmly, if not comfortably, in his arms.

The fact that he was protecting her from *herself*

crossed his mind, but it didn't matter now. He'd made his decision and he was going to stick with it.

"Well, you've got family here, son," Jenn's grandfather said firmly. "Any friend of Jenn and Scotty's is always welcome here."

To his surprise, Johnny found himself fighting a burning sensation in the back of his eyes. He'd thought he'd put aside all his hurt and anguish at having grown up without a family, but Jenn's grandfather's words pierced his heart.

Johnny wasn't a crying man. He hadn't shed a single tear since he was five years old and his bully of a foster brother had beaten him up for being such a sissy.

He grit his teeth against the onslaught of emotion, determined to overcome it by sheer strength of will but entirely unable to speak.

"That's right, honey," Auntie Myra said, ruffling Johnny's hair as she would a young boy. "Now that you're dating our precious Jenn, you've got to consider us all your family. And I expect you to call me *Auntie Myra.* I know the rest of my family feels the same— *Granny, Granddad.*"

Johnny opened his mouth to speak but only a choking sound emerged.

Auntie Myra held up her hands, thinking he was trying to beg off. If only she knew.

"No, no, we won't hear of anything else, will we, folks?"

Her family clamored over each other to be the first to agree.

Jenn's mother placed a hand on Johnny's shoulder. "I know you must be feeling a little overwhelmed right now, Johnny. Don't let them frighten you away. I know you and Jenn are just dating. You probably haven't made any long-term plans."

That was an understatement. He and Jenn hadn't gotten so far as to what they were going to do in the next minute, much less the next two weeks. Johnny swallowed hard and nodded.

"Still and all, things being the way they are, Jenn's father and I would be honored if you would treat us like family, even if it's just for these two weeks."

Johnny looked at Jenn. Her bright blue eyes were shimmering with unshed tears, from joy or chagrin he couldn't say.

For himself, Johnny thought this might be the happiest moment of his life, and it was certainly going to be the best two weeks he'd ever spent.

He was still feeling guilty about deceiving these kind people, but it was really only a sin of omission, wasn't it?

Anyway, he was already committed. In for a penny, and all that. For the next two weeks, he decided, he was going to toss away guilt and savor every moment.

Because for the first time in his entire life, he had a *family.*

"We need to make some ground rules," Jenn said firmly, as she showed Johnny to his room. "Since *you've* decided to play this little game." Her tone was both defensive and accusatory.

"You started it," he reminded her, then clamped his jaw shut as he realized he sounded like a five-year-old bantering with a sibling.

Jenn Washington was most *definitely* not his sibling.

His grip on his saddle pack increased with every step. Maybe this wasn't such a good idea after all.

"It's true. I did," she admitted quietly after a moment's pause.

At least she had the maturity to own up to her part in this charade. Johnny respected her for that.

"What I don't understand is why you decided not to call my bluff," she said, gesturing him into a small corner bedroom.

Johnny quickly scanned the room. There was a neatly made twin bed with a colorful quilt folded at the bottom, a writing table which faced one of two windows, and a clothes rack in lieu of a closet.

There wasn't space for a closet, or anything else, for that matter. Johnny had to duck his head to get through the doorway.

He set his saddle pack against the foot of the bed and then sat down, feeling less awkward sitting than standing. He looked at Jenn expectantly, wondering if she was going to keep on about the subject of why he hadn't called her bluff, or if she would move on to something else.

Thankfully, it was something else. "I apologize for the cramped quarters. This is the only spare guest room we have left."

"Not a problem," Johnny assured her.

"You're positive you won't be claustrophobic? You're used to sleeping under the stars, I'm sure."

He didn't think now was the time to mention he'd shared a dorm room smaller than this in college. "Like I said, I'll be fine. If I get the hankering, I have my bedroll. I can always go out by the barn and sleep under the stars." He winked at her.

"Yes, I suppose you can," she agreed with a smile. "And then come back inside for a hot shower in the morning. What a novel idea for a cowboy."

Actually, he *was* looking forward to sleeping inside again, on a real bed, and most especially taking a hot shower every morning, but he didn't tell her that. He just grinned.

"Now, back to my original statement. Ground rules," she reminded him. "And I still want to know why you decided to masquerade as *my* Johnny."

"That's a simple answer," he replied, opening the frilly blue gingham curtains to let in what was left of the sunshine. Since the window above the authentic pinewood writing desk faced east, he knew he'd see a lot more of the sun come morning.

He grinned. "I've never had a family. You've just given me two weeks with one. It'll be a new experience for me."

He was surprised when she didn't smile back, but rather frowned at him. "Are you serious? You want to be a part of *my* family? You've spent more than five minutes in their combined company. Are you nuts?"

"You don't know what you have."

Jenn went silent. He *was* serious. And she felt sorry for him. She might not see them often, but she *had* family, and as curious as they were, she knew she could count on them, no matter what.

Johnny, on the other hand, had no one.

He returned to his saddle bag and flipped open the top, taking out a well-used leather-bound bible and placing it on the writing desk, his hand lingering over the cover.

"You're a Christian?" she asked, more alarmed than surprised.

He looked her straight in the eye. "Yes, ma'am. Does that bother you?"

Jenn looked away from his soul-piercing gaze. "No, not at all," she said with forced enthusiasm.

"You're in good company here. My family is all out-spoken believers."

She expected he would naturally include her in the statement, but he continued to watch her, assessing her with eyes that gleamed almost black in the twilight of the bedroom.

To her relief, he didn't press the point. Instead, he shifted back to their original quandary.

"You said something about ground rules." That low, soft-spoken voice went straight to her heart. "What did you have in mind?"

"It's not that I don't trust you," she began, and real-ized to her own surprise that she meant it. "But I think we'd both be more comfortable—and believable—if we simply devise and agree to abide by a game plan. That way there won't be as many opportunities for mistakes, faux pas, if you will."

"Okay," he said straightaway, sitting on the corner of the bed and gesturing her to the pinewood chair. "Should I shut the door, do you think, so others can't hear our conversation?"

"No!" Jenn felt a blush rising to her cheeks—again. "That's exactly what I'm talking about. My family is old-fashioned. *I'm* old-fashioned, at least in that respect. This is exactly the sort of behavior I *don't* want—"

She stopped speaking dead in the middle of her state-ment when she looked at Johnny, who'd crossed his arms and was grinning like the Cheshire Cat.

She suddenly realized he was teasing her, which only made her blush all the more.

"Seriously, now," he said. "What is it you think we should—or should *not*—do to make our grand charade a success?"

Jenn had no idea where to start. Her mind was jumbled with thoughts, and not all were about the pretense they were initiating. He was looking at her with an intensity and amusement that sent her mind and heart completely off-kilter.

Johnny merely cocked an eyebrow, waiting.

"Well, I don't think we should spend too much time together alone," she started, and then realized that was exactly what they were doing now. "Of course, my family will expect us to hang out with each other, but let's try to do that when everyone's around."

He nodded, his lips quirking in that adorable smile of his.

"My family doesn't really believe in private time—individual or otherwise—especially during these reunions. They usually have every spare second filled with some amusement or another."

"Sounds good to me."

"It'll drive you crazy by the end of your first week here."

He laughed. "You like your private time, huh?"

"Oh, yes," she agreed instantly. "I have to have some downtime just to recover from all the noise my family makes. Trust me, you will, too."

"Naw." He shook his head. "Other than devotional time, which I usually take early in the morning before anyone else rises, I think I'm good."

"We'll see." This man was far too agreeable, which would normally set her nerves on edge, but for some reason, she liked him all the more for his positive attitude.

"What else?" he asked, leaning back on his hands.

She wondered if his curly black hair was always as ruffled as it was now, or whether it was the result of wearing his cowboy hat all day.

"I would prefer that you not try to delve into my personal business—my private life. I'll respect yours, as well. Naturally, I'll fill you in on the basics, the things you need to know to be *my* Johnny. But at the end of the day, I'm a very private person, and I'd like it to stay that way."

"Of course," he agreed immediately with a firm nod of his head. "Likewise, darlin'."

The endearment left a mark on her heart. She wanted to deny him the right to use a pet name with her, but realized it could work to her advantage, so she said nothing.

She considered what a simple cowboy like Johnny could possibly consider a *private life.* He spent all his time out on the range with *cows,* after all.

Then again, as a social worker, she'd learned the hard way that everyone had secrets. She knew she personally carried more than the usual load. But still...

"Anything else I should know?" he asked, interrupting her thoughts.

"No P.D.A.," she blurted without thinking, and then groaned inwardly. This was going to be much, *much* more complicated than she'd ever imagined.

That quirk of his lips again. She was positive that trait was going to drive her crazy within the space of a week, for better or worse.

"Public Displays of Affection," she clarified.

Johnny chuckled softly, a deep, low rumble in his throat. "I know what P.D.A. stands for. I was just wondering what your family will think if there aren't any. We're supposed to be in love, remember?"

She choked and sputtered for air.

He just grinned. He was baiting her—again, as if he enjoyed making her blush.

Maybe he did.

"You have a point," she conceded slowly. "I suppose there must be *something.* Er—uh—holding hands once in a while would be appropriate, and I g-guess you can put your arm around me from time to time." She hated how she stammered through that sentence, but she couldn't help herself.

"I feel honored," Johnny said, using his fingers to tip the rim of the hat he wasn't wearing. She couldn't tell whether or not he was teasing her again. His voice was serious, but his midnight-blue eyes were dancing with merriment.

She frowned. "I'm serious. And one more thing. Absolutely, positively *no kissing.* Not even so much as a peck on the cheek. Are we clear on that point?"

His gaze widened, and for the longest moment she thought he might object, but in the end he just nodded. "Done," he said firmly.

She let out a sigh. He had no idea of the relief flooding through her. Because, even though she didn't know this man at all, she believed he meant what he said.

She shouldn't. She knew better.

She'd keep her guard up, no matter what. At least

he'd agreed to the ground rules in theory, and her gut instinct was to take him at his word. Time would tell.

At least he hadn't asked for details, or questioned her rules. Most women, she supposed, probably threw themselves at the handsome cowboy. He probably wasn't used to a woman being as reserved as she was.

She wasn't being mysterious, only cautious.

Johnny couldn't possibly understand the truth. No one could.

"Now for the backstory," Jenn said, happy to change the subject. "You know I'm a social worker in Denver, and I know you're a wrangler in Wyoming. I have absolutely no idea how we could possibly—and plausibly—have met."

"That should be an interesting concoction," he said, reaching his arms up and lacing his long, leather-callused fingers behind his neck. "I've been wrangling cows with your brother for a month."

Jenn blew out a breath. "This is impossible," she stated, as she twisted her index finger through her golden curls. "How on earth would I have ever even met a *cowboy*, much less have started dating one?"

Johnny winced inwardly. The way she said *cowboy* said it all. She wasn't the type of woman, Johnny realized, who would be remotely interested in a down-home, backward *cowboy*.

Only, he wasn't a wrangler.

Far from it.

If she knew who he really was...

No. That would ruin everything.

"Well, I'm doubting you took a trip to Wyoming to

hang out with us *cowboys*," he said in a soft drawl, stressing the word with the same emphasis Jenn had given it.

She chuckled. "Hardly."

"Which means I must have come to Denver for some reason." Johnny was starting to enjoy this, concocting this crazy story with her. A small wave of guilt passed through him—not the larger, more convicting stabs he'd had earlier, but more like the ones he'd had as a teenager, afraid he'd be caught sneaking out of his foster parents' house late at night.

He welcomed the adrenaline rush that accompanied the thought. "I don't have any family, so…"

"You were visiting friends," she prompted. "Mutual friends, between you and me, as it turned out. I have a dozen married friends my family knows are always trying to set me up. That wouldn't be so far-fetched."

"We met, were instantly attracted to one another, and have been calling and e-mailing and seeing each other whenever possible."

The *instantly attracted* part wasn't a lie, anyway—at least on his end, Johnny thought. Jenn was beautiful, with her golden curls bobbing about her face and her blue eyes blazing with delight as the two of them solidified their story.

What man wouldn't want to spend a little more time in her company, maybe get to know her better?

She frowned, pursing her lips together in the cutest way, like a toddler who'd been told *no*. "What about Scotty?" she asked with a tilt of her head that sent those curls afloat in the most enchanting way. Johnny was having trouble concentrating on her words.

"What *about* Scotty?" he asked belatedly.

"It seems an obvious enough problem to me. You guys have been together all month. How did our *relationship* slip past my brother? Wouldn't you have said something about it—about me?"

Johnny chuckled. "For someone who studied human behavior, you sure don't know men very well. We don't talk a lot on the range, and when we do, it's not about our *relationships*. Besides, it appears to me he's taken to the ruse as much as anyone here. If he asks about it, we'll handle it. Trust me."

"I can't believe I—*we're* doing this," Jenn said. She sounded a bit hesitant, but Johnny saw the excitement brimming in her eyes.

She had her reasons for playing this out, and he definitely had his own. It was harmless enough playacting. No one would get hurt.

Besides, he was doing her a favor.

Wasn't he?

The fair damsel in distress, rescued by her knight in shining armor—or rather, in well-worn boots and a dusty old Stetson.

He stood and reached a hand to her. "Come on. Let's go out and face the dragon."

Chapter Three

Jenn didn't know what she expected, but obviously she'd come to the wrong conclusion about this cowboy. Dinner that evening, at the big dining room table, with her grandmother's best china and crystal, was enlightening in ways Jenn couldn't possibly have imagined.

One thing was for certain—Johnny Barnes cleaned up well. When he walked in for dinner, he was clean-shaven, dressed in a crisp red Western shirt with pearl snaps, and a fresh pair of blue jeans, held up by a belt fastened with the inevitable oversize buckle that proclaimed he'd won some rodeo event at some point in his past. He'd even scraped the mud off his boots for the occasion.

Jenn found she almost had to pull her jaw off the floor, she was surprised by how good he looked. If Johnny was handsome with a week's worth of sweat and dirt covering him, he was triply so now, and she couldn't take her eyes off him, which of course he immediately noticed, if his teasing wink was any indication.

Jenn wasn't the only woman in the room to notice

him. Auntie Myra, Granny and even, to Jenn's horror, her own mother began complimenting Johnny left and right, not even allowing him to get a word in edgewise.

"My, what a lovely shirt that is," crooned Auntie Myra, hooking an arm through the young cowboy's.

"Thank you, ma'am, I—" Johnny was immediately cut off by Granny.

"And just look at that extraordinary belt buckle. What were you, son? A bronc buster? A bull rider like our Scotty here?"

"A roper, but—"

"And look at that nice square jaw you were hiding under all that scruff," said her mother.

"Amanda," Jenn's father warned, but to no avail.

Johnny just quirked his lips and shrugged. "Yes, ma'am."

"His hat is still dirty," Jenn pointed out, knowing she was grousing but not caring.

Every eye turned upon her, and everyone but Johnny was frowning their displeasure at her comment.

Johnny, of course, was grinning as if she'd just paid him the highest compliment.

She ignored Johnny's smile and shrugged at the rest of her family. Her statement was true, wasn't it?

Why would the man bring his cowboy hat to the dinner table anyway? At least he had the good sense not to be wearing it indoors, which would have set Granny on him like a pit bull on a piece of fresh meat.

Oh, who was she kidding? Jenn sighed inwardly, giving herself a mental shake. She was born and raised on a Wyoming ranch. All ranch hands had their boots and hats permanently glued to them.

"You may hang your hat on that peg over there," Granny said, gesturing to a large pink and blue country pig plaque, with arms made for just that purpose. Scotty's cavalry hat was already hanging from one of the pegs.

After doing as Granny suggested, Johnny returned to the table and pulled out a chair. But instead of seating himself, he offered it to Jenn, and then fussed around her until he was sure she was comfortable.

Playing his part.

And Jenn couldn't have been more uncomfortable. Especially when he leaned down next to her ear and whispered, "I tried to brush my hat to get the grime off, darlin', but I think the thing has near seen its last days."

She didn't know whether it was his warm breath on the nape of her neck, his leathery cowboy scent or the small endearment, but whatever it was, it was nearly her undoing. She shifted uncomfortably in her seat. She wasn't used to being this near a man—any man—and this handsome stranger was far too charming for his own good.

Or hers.

His sitting down next to her didn't help one bit, never mind the cheeky grin and wink he gave her. She knew it was for her family's benefit, but it still made her uncomfortable.

Not for long, though. It was only moments before Johnny was chatting comfortably with her family, making everyone laugh with his silly jokes.

She sighed inwardly, wondering once again what she'd gotten herself into. She was going to be a cowboy's girlfriend for two solid weeks. Why, oh, why, did the man's name have to be *Johnny?*

The family began passing the dishes around, the

cheerful babble of voices never ceasing as they piled their plates full of food. No one picked up a fork, however, not even Jenn's cowboy.

Granddad, seated at the head of the table, cleared his throat, and everyone became silent. With the quiet reverence Jenn remembered from her childhood, her grandfather folded his hands and bowed his head.

"Let us pray," he said, the usual cheerful gruffness for once gone from his voice, replaced by the humble reverence he offered the Almighty.

Jenn followed suit with the rest of her family, though she shot a quick sideways glance at Johnny. He, too, had his head bowed over clasped hands.

Why, Jenn wondered, did Granddad always wait until *after* the food was served to say grace? Her plate was steaming with fresh beef, a pile of mashed potatoes made from scratch, and green beans.

The aroma of the feast was tantalizing and far too delectable to pass up, and Granddad's prayers were often too long and windy, at least for Jenn.

"We thank you, Lord, for all the blessings of this day," her grandfather began. "For the food you have provided, and especially for bringing a guest into our midst. We ask you to be with us this night, and to bless our good fellowship together as a family. In Jesus' name we pray. Amen."

There was a hearty echo of *amens* following the prayer, and Jenn even heard Johnny's rich, deep voice in the chorus.

Jenn hoped Johnny didn't notice that she didn't join in. None of the rest of the family had, to her knowledge, ever noticed, thankfully, not in all the years since high school. Or if they did, they never commented on her lack of enthusiasm for anything related to praising and worshipping God.

It was one of the moments Jenn hated most about these reunions—the constant stream of prayers to a Heavenly Father she had long since stopped believing in. God was a myth, like Santa Claus. She'd gotten over it a long time ago, except here, in the midst of her family, where faith in God was all too real.

And too painful.

Granddad reached for his fork and havoc set in for the next few minutes as everyone sampled the feast and delighted Granny with their praises over her excellent cooking.

Almost everyone had contributed something to the meal. Even Jenn, who never cooked anything in the city, far preferring take-out to a mess in the kitchen, had been coaxed into snapping fresh green beans.

And boy, was she glad of it now. The thing she missed most about her childhood home, other than the family members themselves, was Granny's mouthwatering home-style cooking. These were two weeks she didn't care if the gravy on the mashed potatoes was clogging her arteries. The delicious meal was just too good to pass up.

It wasn't long, though, before the family started chatting, and inevitably, the topic turned rather quickly to Jenn's relationship with Johnny.

Jenn had thought Auntie Myra would lead the way into that territory, but it was Scotty who spoke up first.

"Now I know your secret, buddy," Scotty said with an enthusiastic grin in Johnny's direction.

Johnny wiped his mouth with the edge of his napkin before replying. "Oh, and what secret would that be?"

Scotty chortled loudly. "Why you were off hugging that laptop of yours every time we hit the bunkhouse. You hinted that it might be a girlfriend, but I had no idea it was my own sister."

Johnny shrugged a shoulder, a forkful of beef hanging midair. "You caught me. I was trying to get to know this pretty young lady better. Tough to do when we're riding the range."

"My sister," Scotty said, sounding amazed. "And I never guessed it."

Johnny winked at Jenn.

"How *did* you two meet?" This time it *was* Auntie Myra doing the questioning, or rather, Jenn thought with amusement, the interrogation.

Jenn thought Johnny would field the question as he had the others, but he nudged her with his knee under the table. Apparently he thought it was her turn to do the talking.

Jenn smiled sweetly at Johnny but nudged him back. Hard.

"We met through mutual friends," she explained. "Really, it all started as a joke."

"A joke?" Johnny queried. Jenn nudged him again with her knee. *He* wasn't supposed to be asking any questions here.

"Well, yes, of course." She looked deeply into Johnny's eyes, sending him a silent warning to shut up and go along with her. "Mark and Julie were always nagging me, wanting to set me up with one of their friends or another. I don't know why young married couples always think they need to share the wealth. Mark and Julie are happily married, so they assume I need to be, as well."

"Hear, hear," called Granny, holding her glass of iced tea in the air in a mock toast and making everyone at the table burst out in laughter.

"In any case, I finally gave in to their pressure and said I would meet one of their friends, on the condition that it be at their house, with them present."

Johnny jumped in at that point. "I didn't know anything about it," he said, lifting his right palm out as if taking an oath.

Jenn's eyes blazed intensely at Johnny before she forced a sickeningly sweet smile to her lips for his benefit more than that of her family. She wasn't going to let him fluster her—not when so much was at stake.

"I arrived early," Jenn broke in. "I think Mark and Julie planned it that way. So there I was, sitting on the sofa with Julie, when this man came in."

Everyone's eyes were riveted on hers.

Even Johnny's.

And, as unusual as it was, not a single family member was speaking. Jenn started to enjoy spinning this yarn, though she still felt a little guilty for misleading everyone.

"I took one look at him and panicked. I thought my friends had gone completely crazy."

"Because he was a cowboy?" Granny asked.

"Oh, no," she said with a cheeky grin. "It was because he was short, bald, wore little round spectacles which looked like they'd come from the last century, and spoke with the highest-pitched, squeakiest voice I've ever heard in my life."

The laughter in the room was deafening.

"Who was he?" Johnny asked curiously, then cleared his throat and continued, "I haven't heard this part of the story before."

Jenn chuckled, ostensibly about the story, but actually because of Johnny's very truthful comment. Of course he hadn't heard the story. He couldn't have, since she was making it up on the spot.

"The bald man turned out to be a neighbor, just dropping in to say hi and return something he'd borrowed, I think." She beamed at Johnny for her family's benefit. "I cannot tell you how relieved I was to hear another knock at the door and see this tall, good-looking cowboy strutting in as if he owned the world."

Johnny ruffled his fingers through his thick, dark, curly locks. "Wow," he exclaimed. "I cannot say how truly thankful I am at this moment for this full head of hair of mine."

If the story were true, Jenn thought, it might even have happened that way, Johnny being a cowboy or not. He was incredibly handsome in his nice, clean Western clothes, though she did wonder momentarily what he might look like in a business suit, his curls tamed with a palm full of hair gel.

But, no. That wouldn't be Johnny; and at the moment, Jenn wasn't sure she'd change him if she could. He was as wild and free as the Wyoming range, and he most definitely looked that way.

Oddly, Jenn found she couldn't complain.

She realized she'd abruptly dropped her story with her daydreaming when Johnny picked it up.

"I don't know for sure how it was for Jenn that night,"

he said, smiling softly down at her, "but for me, at least, the moment our eyes met, I knew beyond the shadow of a doubt that I was a goner."

Her gaze met Johnny's at that moment, as if their story had been true. His midnight-blue eyes were shimmering with amusement and just a touch of something else Jenn couldn't quite identify. Then his mouth did that cute little twist and Jenn thought, if the circumstances she'd concocted were true, *she* might have been a goner, as well.

Even with her past. Even with her secrets.

Johnny was getting to her somehow, and she took a mental step backward, bolstering the defenses she'd relied on all her life.

She didn't want to go there—to the past. And she wasn't about to let Johnny, with his good looks and charming ways, take her there.

Johnny wondered why Jenn's smile had turned so quickly to a frown, and he redoubled his efforts to make the light come back into her eyes.

That she had been hurt in the past, by someone or some circumstance, was a given. She was all bottled up inside. He could see it through her eyes even now, though her gaze had become distant.

The clatter of a fork against a fine china plate interrupted his thoughts. "Love at first sight," exclaimed Auntie Myra. "It's so romantic. Was it that way for you, too, Jenn?"

"Myra," Granny snapped, "don't push the young people. It's their story. Let them say what they want to say."

"Indeed," Jenn's mother agreed. "By all means, go on. We're all anxious to hear the rest of the tale."

Even Jenn's father and grandfather nodded at that statement.

Jenn went from dark to light in a split second, startling Johnny more than he realized. Did lying come so easy to her? She definitely had a knack for storytelling, and she was a phenomenal actress, for her eyes now held warmth toward him.

It almost felt like love, not that he had any experience in that area. He'd never found a woman who instigated the bevy of emotions coursing through him. Whatever he was feeling, it disconcerted him until he could hardly think.

"Just like the love songs paint it, I'm afraid," Jenn admitted with a wink. "Take a look at him," she said, smiling up at him and brushing a stray lock of hair off his forehead with the tips of her fingers. "Who could resist him?"

Johnny swallowed hard. The simple touch of her fingers running through his hair made his heart jump into his chest, thudding so rapidly he thought everyone at the table might hear it.

Jenn *was* a beautiful woman. What man wouldn't be attracted to those bouncy golden curls and bright blue eyes so full of life and intelligence?

But he was getting off-track, and fast.

He reminded himself mentally that her actions were for her family. Part of the ruse and nothing more. Her touch had seemed somehow intimate, yet he knew it was all for show.

It meant nothing. So why did he feel like it did?

"Our dinner together was a bit awkward, with us gawking at each other across the table," Jenn said, punctuating her sentence with a laugh that, at least to Johnny's ears, sounded forced. "I think Mark must have kicked Johnny underneath the table a couple of times to keep the conversation flowing."

Johnny winced visibly, then gave a rueful grin.

"He walked me to my car afterwards," Jenn said, as Johnny slid his arm around the back of her chair. "Talk about cliché."

"He snuck a kiss!" Auntie Myra exclaimed, slamming both her palms down on the table in her excitement, making the silverware and glasses nearest to her dance. "How incredibly romantic!"

"He did no such thing," Jenn protested, with a shake of her head.

Johnny winked at her, but he couldn't help that a tiny bit of his male pride was bruised by her harsh statement. Due to the fast pace of his career and nonstop working obligations, he hadn't dated much in the past few years, but did she really believe kissing him would be so terrible?

"He remarked on how pretty the stars were that evening, and then he asked if he could call me sometime."

"Well, ya obviously gave him your number, didn't ya?" teased Scotty.

Jenn scowled at her younger brother. "I didn't have to," she stated bluntly. "He'd already gotten it from Mark and Julie on the sly."

Granny snickered behind her hand. "Quick thinking, young man."

"Of course, Johnny was busy," Jenn continued. "We spoke on the phone a few times—when *he* called, that is—the man never did give me his telephone number, no matter how many times I nagged him about it. Mostly we've gotten to know each other through e-mail."

The statement shook Johnny like an earthquake. The way she described their meeting—that's exactly how it would have happened, *if* it had happened, for he certainly couldn't have given her his telephone number for where he *really* lived.

Unless he told her the truth about his identity. Unless she knew who he really was.

Maybe if things had been different…

He shook his head mentally. This was nothing but a charade. He needed to get his head back on his shoulders, and right quickly.

Auntie Myra held her hands to her cheeks. "This is so romantic. I think I may faint."

"Oh, knock it off with the dramatics already, Myra," Granny snipped.

His supper finished, Jenn's grandfather pushed back his chair and stood. "Seems to me," he said with a slow drawl, "that given the circumstances, we ought to be giving these two youngsters some alone time."

Jenn's eyes widened. Johnny quickly slipped his arm from the back of the chair to her shoulders, where he gave her a reassuring squeeze. He was certainly aware she hadn't concocted this story in order to spend time with him—alone. She'd made that perfectly clear.

"I think that's a fine idea, don't you, darlin'?" Johnny asked softly. "Maybe Jenn and I could take a walk. It's a nice night out, now that the temperature has dropped some. She could show me around the ranch a bit, help me get my bearings."

"Sure," Jenn agreed, sounding, at least to Johnny's

ears, quite reluctant. Then she chuckled, surprising him with her sudden change in spirit. "Maybe Johnny can comment on the stars again."

That got the family laughing.

"Just be sure and get *his* telephone number this time," Scotty teased. "'Course, there ain't no cell phone service out on the range."

Jenn shrugged. "So I'll get his house number. He has to go home sometime."

Johnny cringed inwardly until his gut was in knots. The last thing he wanted to think about was going home. He rose to his feet and offered Jenn his hand. "Let's go see those stars."

Jenn took his hand, but dropped it the moment she was standing. She strode to the door, not even looking back to see if Johnny was following.

Johnny barely made it out the door after Jenn before he threw back his head and laughed heartily. "Darlin', you really know how to spin a story."

Jenn scowled and turned away from him, wrapping her arms around her, both for warmth and the sense of protection it offered. "Do you know what I just did?" she ground out from between clenched teeth.

"No. What?"

Jenn turned to him, her chest squeezing so tight she thought she might suffocate. "I just lied to my family."

Johnny frowned. "Yes, *we* both did."

Jenn shook her head. "It bothers me. I know I started it with that whole sending-myself-flowers thing, but I never dreamed I would end up creating an entire backstory to go along with the flowers. I feel so awful about deceiving everyone. They asked, and the words just flew out of my mouth before I could think about them."

"I understand," Johnny said softly. "You were under a lot of pressure there."

"But I shouldn't have made up a story. I should have told them the truth."

"Yes," Johnny agreed. "The truth is always best. But even without words, we've been lying to your family since the moment I walked in the door."

Jenn clutched at her chest, which was still spasming so erratically she couldn't take a proper breath. "What did I just do to the two of us?"

Johnny shrugged and shook his head but didn't offer any kind of answer, not that Jenn really expected him to. It was right there in front of them both, whether spoken or unspoken.

"I've buried us, that's what," Jenn said with another scowl.

Johnny blew out a breath. He hadn't been prepared for the way Jenn's family had questioned them over dinner, though he realized now he should have been. Jenn's family was boisterous and openly curious. They were bound to ask questions about his and Jenn's relationship.

Johnny hadn't been ready at all, and Jenn had simply panicked and spun a quick yarn to ease them out of a tense situation. He certainly couldn't lay the blame at her feet. He didn't want to. It was at least as much his fault as it was hers.

But no matter how he cut it, what they'd done was still lying, wasn't it? What did it matter who said the actual words?

Guilt weighed heavily on Johnny, as it obviously did

on Jenn. He wasn't sure *what* the right thing to do was at this point. If they went and told the truth, *he'd* have to tell the truth about who he was.

He wasn't ready to do that. Not for him, and definitely not for Jenn's sake. He knew he was being stubborn and bullheaded, but he also knew, without asking, that Jenn was purposefully shielding herself from something, and hiding it from her family.

The problem was, he couldn't straight-out ask Jenn what was wrong. He wanted to support her, he just wasn't sure how. She'd made the rules, after all.

"I don't know what to do now," Jenn admitted in a coarse, conspiratorial whisper.

Instinctively, Johnny put his arm around her shoulder. Surprisingly, she didn't shrug him off. "I don't know, either, Jenn. Maybe we should pray together about it, seek God's wisdom on how to straighten this mess out."

She turned sharply and slipped out of his grip, moving to face him. "Can we just take a walk?" she suggested instead.

Johnny didn't miss the way she changed the subject, any more than he'd missed the way Jenn hadn't been praying at the table tonight.

Yet they'd talked about their faith in God, hadn't they? She'd asked if he was a Christian right off the bat, and he knew how much her family valued their faith.

But what had she said in response? Had she mentioned her own faith? Johnny racked his brain for the answer but couldn't seem to remember. He'd been distracted then by Jenn's presence, just as he was distracted now. The woman made his senses all topsy-turvy.

"Where are we going?" he asked, as she turned and started trekking toward a meadow.

"Just out—under the stars, like we supposedly did before," she said gruffly. "There isn't much to show you that you haven't already seen a million times. You've seen one Wyoming ranch and you've seen them all," she joked dryly.

Finally she stopped walking. They were in the middle of a meadow, with dry, waving grass in every direction. "Well, here they are, Johnny."

"What?" he asked, momentarily confused by her train of thought.

"All the stars, in country-evening Technicolor. I knew you'd want to see them. Again." She laughed at her own joke, but it sounded forced.

"It was a great story," Johnny said, catching up with her and grabbing her elbow to turn her toward him. "Maybe it could have been that way. I mean, if we'd met like you said."

Jenn looked at him for a long, silent moment before answering.

"Yes," she said at last, nodding her head ever so slightly. "Maybe it could."

Chapter Four

Morning came, and with it the dreaded announcement that this was *picnic day,* a yearly ritual that filled Jenn's heart with immense trepidation. Swimming was the main attraction, something Jenn dreaded in the worst way. At least she was spending quality time with her family.

And Johnny.

She couldn't get the cowboy off her mind, no matter how hard she tried. She was treading on dangerous territory and she knew it.

This morning he was wearing black jeans and a maroon snap-down Western shirt rolled up at the sleeves. With his boots and hat, of course. What cowboy would be seen without them?

Hardly picnic-by-the-lake attire, Jenn thought with an inward smile, but no doubt Johnny would change into something more appropriate as soon as he heard the family's plans for the day.

Jenn, on the other hand, would be sweltering in her clothes—jeans and a long-sleeved Western shirt she kept snapped at the wrists. And unlike Johnny, she wasn't going to change her outfit, however desperately she wanted to. It was simply out of the question.

End of subject.

His well-used hat was at his side, but it looked like he'd made an attempt, anyway, to dust off his boots.

And his smile was just for her as he pulled out her chair, then went to claim her a cup of coffee from the counter. He was so polite and incredibly dashing. She hadn't been this attracted to a man since—well, she'd never been this attracted to a man before. In fact, she'd gone out of her way to avoid feelings like these.

"One sugar, right?" he asked solicitously. "My darlin', the sweet tooth."

Her breath caught in her throat at his gentle endearment. She didn't *want* to like Johnny. She still couldn't see why she was attracted to him, yet the enticement was definitely there.

But why?

Johnny was everything she didn't want in a man. Cowboys were too attached to their horses and their freedom to give their lifestyles up for the boxed-in atmosphere of school.

And Johnny was the epitome of everything wrangler, from his hat to his spurs. He was rough-cut and rugged. He carried a day's growth of beard on his chin, not clean-cut and clean-shaven as she preferred, or at least she'd *thought* she preferred, until she'd met Johnny. He wore a cowboy's jeans, faded T-shirts under worn Western shirts and dusty boots. She'd always preferred seeing men in crisp business suits and ties.

But that wasn't the point at all, was it?

What was she thinking?

So what if he appeared to be well read and up on current events, and able to playfully banter with her family as if he'd been there all his life. So what if her heart lit up like a candle every time he smiled at her?

The fact was, Jenn didn't want a man.

Any man.

She shuddered as the thoughts and memories she'd kept buried deep within threatened to burst out and overwhelm her once again. She felt a moment of panic, before—with all her will—she crammed those memories back where they belonged, out of sight and out of mind.

She was a woman now—a strong woman, not the foolish girl who'd once let her romantic notions lead her into the worst kind of trauma.

She wouldn't go there, not even for a moment. But it was a sharp, painful reminder to keep her distance from Johnny, both physically and emotionally.

A reminder she clearly needed. Johnny had her head and heart all out of whack. She needed to keep her distance, or she was going to be in even more trouble than she already found herself.

She placed her head in her hand and groaned. How had her life become so complicated? In Denver, she was a respected social worker. She threw herself into her work so she didn't have to think about things like this, didn't have to expose herself to the danger of really feeling anything for anyone.

Out here in the country, there was too much time to think. She rubbed her temples with the tips of her fingers. She almost wished there *was* a God, that she could find it in her heart to believe in a Higher Power with more control over her life than she had herself—which amounted to zero. Despite her best efforts to the contrary, her life was a roller-coaster ride, and she couldn't get off even if she wanted to.

The worst part of it was, she wasn't even sure she wanted to get off. What kind of convoluted nonsense was that?

Maybe God could sort things out, if she believed. It would definitely be simpler if she were a believer, in this household where faith in God was as natural as breathing to most of its occupants.

As natural as breathing. Except to her.

Johnny slipped into the chair beside her, with his own steaming mug of coffee. He grinned at her extended family milling all around the kitchen. "So, what's on the agenda for today?" he asked.

"A picnic," Scotty said, sitting down opposite Johnny and Jenn. "We have one every year, out by the lake. It's one of the highlights of the reunion. You'll love it."

Johnny raised an eyebrow. "Speedboats and jet-skiing in Wyoming?"

Granny chuckled. "It ain't that kind of lake, son. More a grand puddle of mud most of the time, but good enough to splash in and cool off in the hot July sun. And what we lack in water, we make up for in food."

"Granny, you know the way to a man's heart, now, don't you?" Johnny asked, patting his fit stomach for emphasis. "You'd have caught me hook, line and sinker with that delicious cooking of yours…that is, if my heart wasn't already stolen by this young lady here." He tipped his head at Jenn.

Granny blushed. She actually blushed!

"You can stop with the flattery already, young man," Granny teasingly scolded. "All that is going to get you is a big bellyache from me forcing more food down your gullet."

"Oh, there won't be any force necessary," Johnny assured the elderly woman.

Jenn cringed, not so much from Johnny's words as the reminder of the picnic. As much as she loved Granny's cooking, Jenn would much rather partake of the delicious meal at the comfort of the dining room table. Jenn adjusted her shirt over her jeans and composed herself.

There were too many lies, too much deception. But she'd done it before—for years—and this time would be no different.

Except for Johnny. The cowboy presented her with a whole new set of difficulties.

A whole new set of *lies.*

She had her reasons. She'd simply do what she'd always done—sit in the shade of a tall cottonwood tree and pretend she was relaxing. That she didn't want to swim.

And hope Johnny would buy her story. For some reason, she was more worried about being found out by this relative stranger than she was by her very own family.

It wasn't long before they were on their way to the picnic grounds. All of them were on foot, as the lake was less than a mile's hike. Even to Jenn, who was in a decidedly bad mood, the day was lovely: not a cloud in the sky, and a refreshing breeze coming in from the west. Wyoming was, she had to admit, beautiful country.

She wondered why she had hated it so very much when she was a teenager.

She had wanted only to leave. Now, older and more mature, she saw what she had missed when she was younger, the peace the rest of her family so loved and cherished.

Jenn sighed and wiped off a trickle of sweat that was drizzling down from the nape of her neck and down her back. Everyone was dressed to swim. Even Granny was geared up in a frilly one-piece bathing suit and matching umbrella to keep off the sun.

Jenn was out-and-out jealous. She tried to direct her thoughts to more pleasant subjects and not on how uncomfortable she was in her warm clothing.

Lost in her own thoughts, Jenn lagged behind, and Johnny, toting the largest and heaviest of the picnic baskets—at his own insistence—slowed his pace to match hers.

Something was wrong with Jenn today, but Johnny couldn't quite put his finger on the problem. The one observation he could make with any surety was that Jenn was the only one in her family not dressed for a good, fun-filled splash in the lake.

She was going to swelter in the heat, he thought; but then again, he might be accused of that, as well. He'd not changed his clothes, but rather wore his swimming trunks underneath his jeans.

Johnny at least had a good excuse for dressing as he did. Since he only had cowboy boots with him, he knew he'd look like a laugh-out-loud dork, walking around in his swimming trunks and a pair of cowboy boots.

Johnny chuckled just thinking about it, and Jenn looked up at him, questioning him with her gaze.

Johnny shrugged. "I was just thinking how hot I am," he explained.

Jenn sighed loudly. "You and me both," she agreed, running the back of her hand against her glistening forehead. "It must be at least ninety degrees out here in the shade."

"I would have worn my swimming trunks, except that I don't have any shoes except my boots here. Can you imagine?"

Johnny smiled when his comment brought a tiny but genuine laugh from Jenn.

"You could have asked Scotty. I'm sure he has an extra pair of sneakers lying around someplace."

Johnny glanced down at his boot-clad feet. "I would have, except my feet are about three sizes larger than Scotty's. I'd never even get my toes into a pair of his shoes."

Jenn's glance fell to his boots, as if considering what he said. "Yes, you're probably right. Scotty always had small feet, even when he was little."

"Is that a nice way of not telling me I have huge feet?" he joked.

"Not at all," she said immediately. "I'd never say something like that."

"You'd think it, though," he teased.

She grinned and shrugged. "Maybe."

"You, on the other hand, had the good sense to wear a comfortable pair of flip-flops." *That was something, anyway,* Johnny thought, though he didn't voice his observation aloud.

So why the rest of her getup, he wondered? It didn't make any sense. Shorts and a T-shirt would have been way more comfortable.

Jenn didn't offer an explanation, though she already looked hot and tired, and the smile she gave him faltered on her lips.

He smiled back but didn't break the silence with questions, no matter how curious he was. She'd asked for privacy in her personal life, and he supposed that included what she decided to wear to a family picnic. He would respect her wishes. If she wanted to tell him anything, she would.

Still, she looked miserable, so he took her hand with his free one and linked her fingers with his. He knew he was taking an enormous chance with that action, with all that *public display of affection* stuff she had spouted at him the first day, but he wanted her to know he was there for her if she needed him.

Besides, it wasn't like he didn't notice her family's transparently obvious glances back at the two of them, no doubt perceiving them as a young couple in love. Surely, they expected to see some sort of friendliness between the two of them.

To Johnny's surprise, Jenn didn't pull away, and they walked quietly, their hands linked, for several enjoyable minutes, until they hiked over the top of a low incline and Johnny spied the lake. While it wasn't waterskiing material, it was larger than he had imagined it would be, and was the deep, dark blue of western water. He couldn't wait to take a cool dip. He was roasting alive in his shirt and jeans.

"Let's set our picnic blanket up there, under the cottonwood trees," Jenn suggested, pointing to the trees and glancing up at him with a forced smile.

Johnny noted that the spot she'd chosen was some distance from where her family was setting up for their picnic, but he followed silently when Jenn tugged on his hand, leading him away from the family, whose company he so enjoyed.

Still, it made sense, he supposed, that the two of them, he and Jenn, would choose a spot with a little bit of privacy, after all. If there was a real relationship between them, that's what Johnny would have wanted to do, he realized. And the thought of spending more time getting to know Jenn wasn't so bad, either.

"They're going to need this," Johnny said, lofting the large wicker basket onto his shoulder. "I think most of the food is in here. They're going to come after us and toss us in the lake if we keep all Granny's awesome cooking to ourselves."

He heard Jenn's soft laughter as he strode down the hill and placed his basket with the others. Everyone was milling about and chattering and laughing as they prepared blankets and set up Granny's umbrella, which would look more at home on a sandy California beach than on Wyoming's rough terrain.

He grabbed a couple of gigantic roast beef sandwiches, loaded with all kinds of extras, from fresh purple onions to ripe tomatoes, two apples and a couple of sodas, then tucked them in his shirt and strode back up the hill to Jenn. She was in the midst of spreading a red plaid blanket across the ground.

Aching for relief from the burning sunshine, Johnny dumped his culinary treasures onto the blanket in a heap and reached for the front of his shirt, popping all the snaps at once with one good, hard yank.

He had a black T-shirt underneath his Western shirt, but Jenn's shocked expression made him feel he'd done something completely inappropriate.

He'd never figure out a woman's mind and moods if he lived to be two hundred years old. He shook his head at her, and then shed the long-sleeved shirt entirely.

"Why did you dump our food like that?" she asked in an accusatory tone.

He raised a brow at her. "Because I'm frying in this sunshine and I want to get out of this hot shirt and jeans. Don't you think you should do the same? Half your family is already splashing at the water's edge."

"You shook up the pop cans when you threw them that way. We won't be able to open them for an hour now."

Johnny met her gaze but was unable to read her thoughts. She'd completely ignored his suggestion and continued harping on one silly action he'd made.

Maybe this was why he'd avoided having a girl-friend. A woman could make a guy go crazy.

Hoping to distract her from the shaken soda and whatever else was bothering her, Johnny hopped around on one foot, trying to remove one of his cowboy boots, thinking his antics might amuse Jenn.

Her look hadn't changed. She was still scowling, her arms wrapped about herself as if she were trying to fend off the cold. *In this heat?*

Suddenly, in one fluid movement, she stood from where she had seated herself on the blanket. Wide-eyed, Jenn backed away from him. She looked disori-ented, like she wasn't quite seeing what was really before her, but some kind of nightmare behind the shadow of her eyes.

Johnny opened his arms in a gesture of friendship but she didn't seem to notice. When he stepped forward, she backed up. One step, then another, until Jenn was backed against the firm, thick trunk of the cottonwood tree shading them from the heat.

"What are you doing?" she asked, her voice cracking with strain. Johnny knew it was obvious, and he'd already said as much. He was just following the lead of the rest of her family, and getting ready to splash in the cool comfort of the lake.

But for some reason, he realized suddenly, his actions had been taken wrong. And it wasn't him dumping their lunch into an unglorified heap on the picnic blanket, either.

Jenn looked like a little filly ready to bolt, and he knew if he didn't somehow save this situation now, it was going to get out of control in a hurry. He might never win back the peaceful coexistence he and Jenn had formed on the walk over to the picnic site, and that bothered him more than he cared to admit.

He had to act now.

Johnny stepped forward slowly, closing the gap between them. "I was just getting comfortable," he explained gently, though he'd already voiced the words once. Somehow, he knew he needed to say them again in order for her to really hear them. "Jenn, I don't understand. Why aren't you doing the same?"

Jenn shook her head vehemently. "I don't, uh— swim," she said with a quiver in her voice.

Everything inside Johnny made him want to reach for her to give her a reassuring hug, but he sensed she'd balk. It was in her eyes. Instead, meeting her gaze squarely, and moving with infinite care, he placed his hand on the tree, just over her head, ignoring the roughness of the bark cutting into his palm.

He'd just backed her into a corner, figuratively speaking, and they both knew it; but he'd also given her a chance to retreat if she wanted to, to duck under his arm and run away from him and whatever it was that was bothering her so.

Johnny was surprised and relieved when she didn't budge, though her fingers clutched at the tree behind her, as if for support. She was looking everywhere except at him. The sky, the ground, his boots.

Just not his eyes.

With his free hand, he tipped her chin so she had no choice but to meet his gaze. "Don't be frightened," he said, the words tumbling out of his mouth before he could stop them.

Her blue eyes blazed with indignation. "I am *not* frightened," she ground out, brushing away his hand from her cheek.

There was a long, silent pause as they just looked at one another, sizing each other up. Johnny was just trying to figure out what she was thinking, how she was feeling.

Something had set her off, and he still had no idea what it was.

"I would never hurt you," he continued, knowing the words needed to be said, even if she didn't want to hear them.

There was another long pause as Jenn stared into his eyes, measuring the strength of his words. Johnny didn't move a muscle, didn't even breathe. Surely, she could see the truth in his eyes.

Then, as quick as it came, the moment passed. Jenn reached up and tipped his cowboy hat over his eyes. "You going to go swimming in that thing?" she asked a little too brightly. "One boot off and one boot on, Deedle Deedle Dumpling…" she teased, and then swiftly ducked out from beneath his arm.

Jenn sat down on the far edge of the blanket and picked up an apple, gnawing in small bites, as if to give her something to do with her hands.

Her chest was rising and falling with rapid breaths. Johnny had promised not to pry into her personal affairs, and he hadn't. Not really. But he could tell he'd shaken her up with his gentle words—words that hit far too close to home, even for him.

Chapter Five

Johnny would never hurt her.

How she knew that, how she could possibly hope to believe it, was beyond her comprehension. Hadn't she learned anything from her past experiences?

Hadn't she heard those words before?

Yet her gut instinct told her this was different. Johnny was a different sort of man than those she'd encountered in the past.

But could she really trust him? Did she dare?

Johnny flipped his hat off his head and tapped it against his thigh with a laugh. "Guess I look pretty ridiculous at the moment, don't I?" he drawled. "One boot on, one off, like you said?"

Not ridiculous, Jenn thought. *Not even limping around in one boot and one sock. Outrageously handsome, perhaps.* Incredibly charming with that easy smile of his, for sure. But she wasn't about to say *those* thoughts out loud, not in this lifetime, so she merely chuckled.

Johnny stretched himself full-length on the blanket,

murmuring something between a groan and a sigh. He picked up one of the sandwiches and unwrapped it, then took a large bite.

"Incredible," he said, still chewing. "I never knew a roast-beef sandwich could taste so good."

Jenn nodded, her face solemn, but smiling inside in a way she'd never felt before. "It's the ambience."

Johnny threw back his head and let out a peal of genuine laughter, a trait that did strange things to her insides. "Did anyone ever tell you that you have a way with words, Jenn?"

"Mmph," she answered. "More than once. Maybe a few times too many."

He laughed again—hearty, free and sincere. It showed in his eyes as much as on his lips.

Jenn glanced down at the lake. Apparently, either her family was finished eating or they'd opted to forego food in favor of the cool water. Everyone, even her grandparents, were splashing around in the shallow lake and laughing raucously, enough for it to be heard all the way up the hill to where she and Johnny sat.

She slid a glance at Johnny, who was also watching her family's antics, the little quirk of amusement on his lips twitching more than once. He appeared to be genuinely enjoying himself as he munched on his sandwich and watched the lake below.

"Don't feel obligated on my account," Jenn said immediately, gesturing to the lake. Johnny hadn't even bothered to finish stripping down to his swimming trunks. He still had one boot on and one off, his legs stretched out on the blanket, one ankle crossed over the other. "Go get yourself cooled off in the lake," Jenn urged. "The water will do you good, and I can see you want to go."

He looked at her for a long moment, then stretched and stood. But instead of divesting himself of his remaining clothing and racing down the hill to the water's edge, Johnny reached for his maroon-colored shirt, slipping it around his shoulders but not buttoning it.

"What are you doing now?" she asked, puzzled, as he hopped around, replacing his other boot on his foot with an exaggerated lack of grace.

He winked at her and slung his hat back on his head, tipping it at her for emphasis. "Swimming is not really my style, anyway," he stated with a negligent brush of his hand. "I'd rather be on a horse."

Jenn's eyes widened in surprise. She could see right through him. There was no doubt in her mind that he was making his decision based on her needs, to make her feel more comfortable at his own expense—and it wasn't any small sacrifice he was making for her. It was way too hot for jeans and long sleeves, as well she knew.

"Johnny, you really don't have to do this," she insisted.

He just shook his head and resumed his stretched-out position on the blanket, hat and all. "Aw, don't worry about it," he drawled softly. "I don't feel fully dressed without my boots and hat, anyhow."

She couldn't tell him how much she appreciated his kind gesture. Full of emotion, her heart welled into her throat and she was certain she couldn't speak, to thank him for his kindness.

Anyway, what would she say? She had no reasonable explanation for her own behavior—at least no explanation she cared to share.

Ever.

So she said nothing, and he appeared to be okay with that.

Johnny and Jenn spent a pleasant few minutes in silence, simply watching her family playing in the water, shouting and laughing. It was odd how comfortable she felt with Johnny, Jenn thought. She could just sit here in silence without feeling the need to speak, and without feeling awkward and needing to fill the void with words.

It was…*peaceful.* Jenn wasn't sure she'd ever felt that way before. She smiled at him and he smiled back, giving her a friendly wink Jenn interpreted as his way of telling her he felt the same way.

Johnny didn't mind sitting quietly with Jenn. Ostensibly, he was caught up in the action below at the lake, but every so often he glanced at the beautiful woman at his side. He couldn't help himself.

What made her tick? Why was she vacillating between hot and cold, like a faucet?

Eventually he broke the silence. While Johnny enjoyed the serenity between them, he wanted to get to know Jenn better, and that required speaking. She was supposed to be his girlfriend, after all. The more he knew about her, the better—for the sake of the charade, of course.

"Tell me about your work," he said, intentionally breaking one of her rules, but hoping she trusted him enough to let it go.

She glanced at him, obviously weighing her options in her mind before she spoke.

At length, she sighed. "I work in the foster care sys-

tem," she said softly. "There are so many needy children
out there. I guess you already know that, with your past
and all. I don't mean to remind you of anything you'd
rather forget. It's just that it frustrates me sometimes that
I am able help so few kids when there are so many out
there."

"Every child matters, Jenn," Johnny said. "You make
a real difference in the world. That's more than I can say
for the work I do."

Jenn laughed, her tone bitter. "Most days, I only see
the bad. It's agonizing and frustrating, but every so often
something wonderful happens and makes all the terrible
stuff worth it."

"Do you have anyone back in Denver to share your
triumphs and disappointments with?"

Jenn shook her head. "So much of what I do as a
social worker is private. Most of the time, I can't talk
about my work at all, and even when I can, it's hard for
me to put into words what I'm doing, and how I'm feeling. I think that's probably a lot of the reason I don't have
many close friends, though I do have a few colleagues I
spend time with. Not that I have much time. My work
schedule doesn't make for much of a social life."

She paused thoughtfully. "It's tough on
relationships—with other women or with men. I can't
seem to create an emotional bond."

"Other social workers find meaningful, fulfilling relationships outside their jobs," Johnny pointed out gently.

Jenn nodded. "True."

"But not you."

"But not me, what?"

She was avoiding the question and they both knew

it, so Johnny didn't push her or try to explain himself. He just waited.

After a while, Jenn blew out a breath. "Yes. You're right. Other people are successful with relationships and I'm not. I just can't seem to connect. It doesn't happen for me. Maybe I've got faulty wiring. I really don't know."

"Give yourself some credit, Jenn," Johnny said softly. "You're special. Anyone who has been around you for more than five minutes knows that. But you're lonely." It was a statement, not a question.

"Oh, no," she protested immediately, with a firm shake of her head. "Not lonely. *Alone.* And it was my choice to make, Johnny. Now, can we drop the subject and move on? I'd ask you what you do for a living, and for fun, I imagine, but I already know you play with cows all day."

Johnny internally winced at her weak attempt at a joke. It hit way too close to home. Wrangling cattle *was* fun for him, but it sure as shootin' wasn't his real job. He didn't want to be thinking about that right now.

Besides, his heart went out to her, feeling her pain as if it were his own. He felt an inexplicable need to help her, to rescue her, though he didn't have any notion as to why he felt that way, or what it was she was trying so desperately to avoid.

When she said the word *alone,* he knew she meant it. He'd watched her at dinner last night as they all politely bowed their heads for grace. Jenn had been the only one who hadn't joined in prayer.

Her whole family appeared to be fervent believers. They thanked God for every good blessing. There was a beautiful wooden cross in the living room over the stone fireplace, and prayer plaques spread on walls throughout the house, even in his own bedroom.

But Johnny deeply sensed there was something different with Jenn, something missing, and he thought he might know what—Who—it was.

He was fishing around for a way to ask her about her walk with the Lord, without it coming off as condescending, when there came sudden shouting from the bottom of the hill. Everyone was crowded around the lake, and Scotty was squarely in the middle. He was waving his hand in the air and then submerging under the water.

The calls from shore sounded to Johnny like those of distress.

He didn't give it a moment's thought. He sprinted down the hill as fast as his legs would pump, taking only a moment to toss his hat on the shoreline before diving into the water.

Jenn stood, mouth agape. What was the crazy cowboy doing? He'd plunged into the water, boots and all, yet was swimming with strong, even strokes toward Scotty.

Didn't Johnny know Scotty was just fooling around? Obviously not.

Jenn skittered down the hill, reaching the bank just as Johnny reached Scotty's side.

"It's okay, you're safe" she heard Johnny call out. Johnny was trying to flip Scotty into a supportive position, to swim them both to shore, but Scotty was fighting tooth and nail to get away from him.

"Just relax and go easy," Johnny coaxed. "I can't help you if you fight me."

Jenn looked around, wondering what she should do. Should she call out to Johnny, let him know Scotty wasn't in any real danger? Or should she just let the scene play out? Either way, in her mind, Johnny was a bona fide hero, always thinking of others before himself.

Her relatives were hooting and hollering for all they were worth, egging Johnny on with their chatter.

And they were laughing.

Jenn couldn't stand by and let her family make fun of a man who would risk his own well-being for someone he'd only known for a short while.

"Johnny," Jenn called loudly. "Stand up."

"What?" he yelled back, submerging momentarily under the water as Scotty continued to struggle in his arms.

"Stand up," Jenn repeated, louder this time. She shaded her eyes from the sun, trying to see what was happening through the brilliant glare of the sun on the water.

Johnny must have understood her words the second time, for he did as she asked. With the man being six-two and the water at six feet in the deepest part of the lake, the waves barely met his hair line.

Everyone was laughing in earnest now, even Scotty, who was playfully splashing water at his wrangler friend.

Everyone, that is, except Jenn.

Johnny hadn't wasted an instant when he thought Scotty was in trouble. He had been there, without a thought for his own safety, and had dashed to the rescue, not guessing for one second he had been hoodwinked.

Now his heroic act was being—albeit playfully—mocked by her family.

Jenn didn't want to laugh at Johnny. She wanted to hug him until he couldn't breathe.

Johnny trudged to shore with his arm draped around
Scotty, bellowing out a full-bodied laugh of his own,
throwing his head back in a way that made Jenn's insides feel like mush. He swept up his cowboy hat, used
his free hand to slick his hair back, and then planted his
hat on his head, low over his eyes.

He looked around at her family, his features unread-
able. Everyone stopped laughing and stared back at
him. Jenn wondered if they were as troubled by their
teasing as he must be. Jenn was appalled and ashamed
of her family's behavior.

Johnny had every right to be angry, or embarrassed,
or maybe a little of both. Surely, his male pride had been
wounded, if nothing else.

Suddenly, Johnny gave a toothy grin and tipped the
edge of his hat with his fingers. "Thank you. Thank you
very much," he said in an absurdly exaggerated Elvis
impersonation.

Even Jenn laughed. How could she not, when Johnny
managed to take even the most uncomfortable circumstance in stride—and with a contagious grin on his face
to show for it.

She and Johnny were as opposite as day and night,
Jenn realized. Jenn fretted over every little issue and was
far too conscious of her own pride. She would have
been fiercely wounded by the kind of cavalier behavior
her family had shown Johnny.

She couldn't just let it go, not like Johnny so very
easily did. What was the cliché? Like water off a duck's
back? That was how Johnny took everything; while
Jenn herself would let that same water drown her.

How were the two of them going to continue with

this act? They were too different in personality to have been genuinely attracted to one another, much less to have tried to make a relationship. Surely, someone would see right through the ruse.

How could they not?

Jenn took a mental step backward, trying to see her family through Johnny's eyes. Clearly, he didn't perceive the incident the same way she did. He was all smiles and laughter.

She looked around at her family, who were still joking and laughing with Johnny.

With Johnny. Not at him. What Johnny was experiencing was genuine and familiar—the loving family life Jenn took for granted. Those things about her loved ones that drove her crazy were the same things making Johnny grin so widely now.

It was an epiphany long in coming. There was much in her life she needed to reevaluate.

But not now, not when Johnny, still sopping wet, moved to her side and dropped a wet arm over her shoulder, giving her a friendly nudge.

He was getting her soaked, and obviously intentionally, at that.

Funny, though, it didn't seem to matter to Jenn as she thought it might. Not when Johnny smiled down at her with his dancing blue eyes and that irritating, adorable quirk of his lips.

Johnny winked at her, then gave the family another broad grin. "Well," he drawled slowly, "at least my hat's dry."

Chapter Six

The following day found Jenn so angry she thought steam must be rushing from her ears. And for once, it had nothing to do with her family boxing her into a corner about faith or relationships. Surprisingly, it didn't even have anything to do with the gigantic mess—and it *was* a mess—she had created with Johnny Barnes, or even the man himself.

It was her stupid, useless, piece of junk laptop computer she was about to chuck out the window and have done with altogether. She'd been fiddling with the uncooperative piece of electrical equipment for over two hours now, to no avail.

Vacation or no vacation, she had work to do, and she was never going to be able to access her files if she couldn't get her worthless computer to work. And with no computer tech within miles around who could help her, Jenn had little hope she'd actually be able to toil through the problem on her own.

She didn't spend any more time with her computer than she had to, preferring her work in the field, with real people. Perhaps she hadn't paid enough attention to the modifications made on her computer so she could access her work on her holiday.

Accessing her files from the wide expanse of Wyoming ranch land had sounded like a piece of cake when the computer tech back in Denver had showed her how it was done. She wasn't a complete illiterate, or idiot, for that matter, where computers were concerned, but at the moment, she felt like one.

Her stupid one-click-of-the-button software wasn't *clicking*.

Now how was she supposed to change that?

Anger was rapidly turning to sheer panic. She had a couple cases she'd left with coworkers, and they weighed heavily on her mind. No matter how long she worked at her profession, she'd never forgotten a single face of those dear, sweet orphaned or abandoned children she worked with. She just *had* to know what was happening on her latest cases, on the off chance she could offer some assistance or advice.

Just to know, really.

A knock at her door startled her so much she nearly jumped out of her seat.

"It's Johnny," came a soft drawl from behind the closed door. "I started to worry about you when you didn't come down for breakfast. Are you feeling okay? Is there something I can do for you?"

Glad to have something to do other than pound her computer into the ground and jump on it until it was smashed in dozens of tiny pieces, she slammed the lid on the laptop, hopped up out of her chair and swung the door open wide.

Apparently, Johnny had been leaning against the other side of the door, for he came crashing into the room off-balance, and swerved right into her desk, slamming his palms down with both hands and nearly sending her computer careening to the floor.

He could have saved his pride, but instead, he saved her computer, snatching it up and hugging it tightly to his chest with both arms before falling ungracefully to the rug on his backside.

Frankly, Jenn thought he should have saved himself and let the computer fall where it may; but she knew voicing her thoughts aloud would do more harm than good at this point, so she remained silent. She couldn't help but smile at the adorable, rumpled picture Johnny made, sprawled out on the floor, hugging her computer, but she hid her grin behind her fist so Johnny wouldn't see.

"Sorry. Sorry," he apologized, righting himself and returning the computer to the desk. "Mercy, woman, you ought to warn a man before you swing open the door like that."

She crossed her arms over her chest and glared at him, though she suspected her eyes were still twinkling with mirth. "You were the one who knocked. If you didn't have the good sense to stand away from the door before I opened it, how is that my fault?"

He didn't have his cowboy hat with him, for once, but he nonetheless tipped the nonexistent brim at her with a conciliatory grin. "Touché, darlin'. You spending some time on your computer? Not doing work on your vacation, I hope."

Not doing work was exactly right, and this time Jenn scowled for real, remembering her recent tussle with the contrary piece of electronic equipment, a fight in which she'd lost by a landslide. Johnny's presence could only make her humiliation all the more viable, so the sooner she got rid of him, the better.

"Okay, first, don't call me darling. Second, if I'm hungry, I'll come to breakfast. If not, I won't. Third— and I think we agreed on this point earlier—you are not my keeper."

Inside her heart, she knew she wasn't being fair to him, ranting like this, but she couldn't seem to help herself. Johnny had simply picked a very, very bad time to come knocking on her door.

"Look, darl—uh—Jenn, your granny sent me lookin' for you. She said you're an early riser and it's not like you not to come down and join the family for breakfast. Everyone was worried about you. That's all."

Jenn ran her fingers against her scalp, attempting to ease the tension headache building there, and not caring if she looked a mess.

"I apologize," she said, because that's what she knew she was supposed to say, and not so much because she was feeling it at the moment. "I'm not angry with you, Johnny, or with my family." She blew out a breath.

This time, when his smile showed amusement, Jenn didn't think it was cute. She wanted to punch his lights out.

She sighed again. No, she didn't. Not really. She wasn't being fair to Johnny, and she knew it. He was just being his same old, likeable, distractingly charming self, even if it was grating on her nerves like crazy at the moment.

"Grrrr," she growled out in barely suppressed frustration. "It's not you, Johnny. It's this dumb, stupid, idiotic computer!"

He lifted a brow. "Seems like a lot of adjectives for that little piece of equipment there."

"Yeah? You try it sometime. That *little piece of equipment* is supposed to interface with my work computer, and I can't even get it on the Internet."

"In the middle of Wyoming? Does that really surprise you, darlin'? I'm half surprised they have a working telephone up here. This pretty much has to be no-man's-land, or something, where the Electronic Age is concerned, don't you think?"

"For my cell phone, yes," Jenn answered, still glaring at her computer. "I never expect to get service way out here. But the computer tech at my office assured me he had me wired up for this dumb, stupid, idiotic piece-of-junk computer."

Johnny chuckled loudly. "There go those adjectives again."

Now she glared at him in earnest. He wasn't helping her mood any with his glib comments. "Okay, so my vocabulary turns to mush when I'm angry. Thank you so much for pointing that out to me."

He threw back his head and laughed—at least, until Jenn advanced on him like a cougar on a rabbit, her hands planted on her waist so she wouldn't be tempted to flat-out strangle the man.

"Whoa, there, darlin'," Johnny said, holding his hands up as if she'd held a gun to his head. "I was only teasing."

With another frustrated growl, she backed off and

slumped into the desk chair. Couldn't he see she didn't need to be teased right now?

Fighting a losing battle with her computer was one thing. Fighting that same battle with the gentle cowboy smiling down at her was another.

He stepped before her and kneeled so he was eye to eye with her. His smile disappeared. "I can be a big dumb ox sometimes," he stated bluntly, his eyes changing to a color that was almost black in its intensity. "Here I am, trampling all over your tender feelings, when I ought to be lending you a hand."

His gaze took the fight right out of her, and his words confounded her. She was afraid to ask, but she did, anyway. "Lending me a hand, how, exactly?"

He chuckled. "I think your exact words were, 'You try it sometime.'"

Her eyes widened. The man couldn't be serious. Okay, sure, Scotty had said he'd seen Johnny with a laptop in the bunkhouse where they wrangled, so he obviously was at least familiar with computers. But almost everyone e-mailed in this age. Fiddling around with a high-tech computer program was another thing entirely.

If she couldn't click the link and make it work, it was highly improbable it would suddenly work for Johnny. Cowboy charm only went so far after all, and she doubted it extended to inanimate objects, she thought, with a grim smile.

"Look, I've already tried everything and then some on that dumb—uh—computer that the tech support guy in Denver said to do. Nothing works. There's nothing you can do about it."

There went those lips again, curling in amusement,

as if she'd said something funny. Which she hadn't. "Don't be so sure about that."

He reached for her computer, but Jenn blocked him. "Look, Johnny, I appreciate what you're trying to do here, but I think it would be better if I just put the thing away and admit defeat."

"Defeat? I didn't think that word was in your vocabulary."

It wasn't. But if it was between that and having some cowboy try his hand at fixing her computer, she'd choose defeat—at least for now. She'd no doubt have the annoying laptop out within the hour, trying once again, and probably unsuccessfully, to make the interface work.

"Why do you need it to interface with your work machine?" Johnny asked softly.

"What?" she asked in confusion, having been abruptly pulled from her own thoughts.

"The interface. Why do you need it? I thought you were on vacation here."

"I am," she said immediately. "It's just that there are a couple cases I'm working on—a couple kids caught in the bureaucracy of the system. I'm kind of worried about them, is all, and wanted to check up on how things were progressing with them."

He reached out a hand to brush the backs of his fingers against her cheek, but she instinctively pulled away from his touch. He dropped his hand immediately, but his eyes were so warm and gentle, it made her insides hurt.

"You really care about these kids, don't you?" he asked in that soft-spoken voice of his.

"Every last one of them," she whispered, her heart tightening with all kinds of emotion.

"Then," he said simply, "let me have a pass at your computer."

"Johnny…"

He reached out his hand again, this time using just his index finger to tilt her chin up just slightly, so there was no way she could turn away from him. As if she could have, anyway. His gaze had locked her eyes to his.

And this time, much to her own surprise, she didn't flinch from his tender touch.

"Trust me," he said softly.

"I do, but…"

"Trust me," he said again.

With effort, she broke her gaze from Johnny's. Elbows on her knees, she buried her face in her hands. She couldn't think straight when she was looking into his eyes like that.

It made absolutely no sense to hand her computer over to this cowboy. He was still a stranger, even if she felt an inexplicable closeness to the man. Her computer tech back home would have her hide.

But then again, what could it hurt? What harm would there be in allowing Johnny to see what she'd already discovered? It wasn't as if he could somehow harm the computer. Johnny would just try the same links, get nowhere and shrug it off.

Shaking her head at the wisdom of her action, she stood and moved out of the desk chair, making a sweeping gesture toward the laptop. "Be my guest. Quite frankly, I'm on the verge of throwing the stupid computer out the window anyway. And I don't think you can break the thing by punching a few keys."

"Yeah, probably not," he agreed, sliding into the seat

she'd vacated. He opened the laptop and stared for a moment at the screen she'd left on—the interface which wasn't working.

"The tech in Denver told me all I had to do was push on this little link here," she said, pointing to the blue line on the screen, "And then my work station desktop was supposed to appear out of nowhere. As you can see, nothing's happening."

Johnny scrubbed his hand through his hair, making his curls go every which direction, then winked at her. "You're right. Nothing's happening..."

She nodded vigorously, just short of saying *I told you so*.

Then he grinned at her. "Yet."

Brushing his hands over the keyboard as if he were a virtuoso pianist about to begin a piano concerto, he began typing at lightning speed. This in itself was an enormous surprise to Jenn—a cowboy who typed eighty words a minute?

Johnny continued to surprise her at every turn, and she wondered what else she didn't know about him. It was worth looking into, she thought—and then she glanced at the computer screen, horror gripping her insides.

Little boxes began appearing and disappearing, and then the screen went black, with only a tiny white cursor blinking in the far upper-left corner.

Jenn wanted to scream. What had the crazy cowboy done to her computer?

"Johnny," she squeaked, her voice barely sounding from her throat. "Please. Just stop."

"Stop?" he asked with a chuckle. "Darlin', I'm just getting started."

With that, he began punching in what Jenn now recognized as computer code—*complex* computer code. Line upon line upon line of it, without stopping for a moment to consider what he was doing.

Jenn didn't know whether to laugh or cry, but one thing she knew for sure—she knew absolutely nothing about the cowboy who called himself Johnny Barnes.

In mere minutes, Johnny had her machine back up and running—and this time, when he pressed the interface link, her Denver work station appeared instantly.

"I made a few modifications," he said with a grin. "That tech you have in Denver isn't as good as he thinks he is."

"M-modifications?" Jenn stammered, staring blindly first at the computer, and then at the handsome cowboy-slash-computer genius.

"Mmm-hmm," he murmured with a low, soft chuckle. "You can now access every file in your system, rather than merely your current caseload. Facts, figures, pictures. It's all there. Your communication system on this computer was a bit outdated. I fixed that, as well. And of course I pumped the speed up for you."

"Of course," she echoed vaguely.

She shook her head to clear her mind, feeling as if she'd just stepped off another planet.

Or else *he* had.

She was in limbo, somewhere between reason and insanity, and wasn't exactly sure which side she was hovering the closest to.

"Johnny, you're a genius," she said at last, laying a hand on his shoulder.

He tipped his imaginary hat again. "Why, thank you, ma'am."

"No, I mean it," she continued. "You have to take me seriously here."

"Darlin', I always take you seriously," he bantered.

Johnny had been there for her, ever since he'd stepped in the door that first day. He'd been doing all the giving in their pseudorelationship, and she'd been doing all the taking. He'd even put up with her bad mood this morning, letting her take verbal swings at him without even trying to hit back.

This was her chance to do something for him—if she could get him to listen to her. She wasn't sure he was paying attention, not with the lazy, catlike grin lining his face and his eyes half-closed.

"You have an extraordinary gift. I have to say, I'm astounded." Jenn shook her head. "Why didn't you tell me you were able to do such spectacular work programming computers?"

He shrugged. "You didn't ask."

"Yes, but don't you see? You're out there herding cattle when you could be making money—*loads* of money—in the computer business. Based on what I've witnessed today, with your talent, you could probably open up your own company if you wanted to, or at least troubleshoot for the big guys."

Johnny frowned and looked away from her. "Money isn't everything, Jenn."

He was missing her point entirely, and her frustration once again began to build. "That's not what I'm saying, or at least that's not all I'm saying. Sure, money is part of it. You can't possibly make a decent living wrangling cattle. But it's so much more than that. Johnny, can't you see you're wasting your God-given talent out there on the range?"

"Am I?" His gaze met hers, this time with an intensity so fierce his eyes were once again almost black in color.

"Just think, Johnny, how much you could benefit. Why—"

"Jenn," Johnny barked, cutting her off. It was the harshest tone she'd ever heard him use, and her gaze widened even as her mouth closed.

"Sometimes," he said slowly—not hesitant, but obviously taking time in selecting the right words, "men choose to be cowboys because they don't want to be involved in any part of the corporate rat race. Not every man wants to spend all his time in a claustrophobic office environment, in some small cubicle with telephone gear practically growing out of his ear.

"Out on the range, a man is a free spirit. No buildings, no commitments, just a man, his horse and the cattle he's herding."

Johnny paused. His gaze had never left Jenn's, and she was blinking back at him with her enormous, glittering blue eyes, looking for all the world as if he'd just said the moon was made of green cheese.

Clearly, she didn't comprehend a word he was saying, and for some indefinable reason, he desperately wanted her to understand his point of view.

But of course she wouldn't get where he was coming from; Jenn thrived on the very life Johnny was trying so desperately to avoid.

And why was he trying to explain himself, anyway?

Why should he care what she thought about him or his genius skills?

But he did care. He cared very deeply. And he wanted her to care, too—not just with a token understanding, but with real appreciation.

That wasn't likely to happen, especially not now, when he'd revealed far more of himself than he ever meant to. Feeling more than a little trepidation, he suddenly realized he'd nearly given himself away this morning, all in an effort to help her.

Who was he kidding? He'd been showing off with his skills in order to impress her in the field he knew best. He been strutting his stuff like the vainest rooster in the barnyard.

Unfortunately for him, it had worked—all too well for his own good.

Jenn had been impressed, all right. Enough to want to send him straight to the corporate prison many people called their lives.

The very life he was trying to escape.

Chapter Seven

Johnny managed to avoid Jenn for most of the day, more because she had locked herself in her room with her computer than because of anything he did. Although, he thought wryly, if he had any sense he'd be out of this house and out of Jenn's life at the first opportunity, before he betrayed himself, or more accurately, exposed his betrayal to a family Johnny had come to hold dear to his heart. Especially Jenn.

But he couldn't bring himself to even consider leaving before his two weeks were up, so he stayed and prayed he wouldn't be found out. With every passing second during the afternoon, Johnny missed Jenn's radiant presence; but even so, he managed to enjoy the cheerful company of her extended family. Granny and Auntie Myra were a riot, bantering back and forth like a couple of old hens.

Even funnier was the way Jenn's grandfather with stood it all with the patience of a saint and the gruff good-nature borne of decades of love.

Love Johnny had never known, and certainly had never seen in action. This family continued to surprise him with their love of God and their affection and support for each other. He was really going to miss them all when he left at the end of next week, to return to the Double Y ranch to finish out his summer as a wrangler.

This was what a family was supposed to be, everything he'd dreamed of in his childhood.

And Jenn?

Well, beautiful, fiery-tempered Jenn was definitely the icing on the cake.

More than likely, he'd never see any of them again in his life, except, of course, Scotty, since they still had another month's work on the Double Y.

Johnny had an ache in his gut so fierce he couldn't even eat a decent supper. He must have looked as green as he felt, for no one commented when he excused himself from the table early.

Marching straight to his room, he grabbed his bedroll and headed for the peace and openness of the starry night sky. He never got tired of lying on his back, stargazing in the depths of Wyoming ranch land. Where he could actually *see* the stars.

Where he was from, the only stars he could make out were the Big Dipper and sometimes Orion's Belt, on especially clear nights. Out here, it was all he could do to *find* those constellations amidst the millions of stars twinkling down on him.

He didn't know when he finally drifted off to sleep, but it was much later in the night. Not even the stars had helped him turn off his racing mind, or ease the throbbing pain in his chest.

When he awoke, it was to Scotty's laughter.

"I'm with you, buddy," the youngster said, sliding down to the ground beside Johnny. "Sleeping inside drives me clear out of my mind."

Groggily, Johnny sat up, shoved his curly mop of hair back with his fingers, and planted his hat on his head, pulling the brim low over his brow on the off chance Scotty might see any of his feelings in his eyes. He cleared his throat before speaking. "Yeah, sport."

"I wish you would've come got me. We could've camped out together."

Johnny chuckled. "Boys' night out?"

Scotty grinned. "Something like that. Why are you out here, anyway? No—I know. They all drive you nuts, don't they?"

"Your family? No. No—they're all great."

"Liar. My sister is especially bad on that count. She jams herself right under your skin like a bad splinter, and just keeps on rubbing so you can't ever forget she's around."

Johnny bit his lip to keep from laughing. *That* much was true, anyway. Scotty's sister was a hard woman to forget about, even for a minute.

"You wanna get away from everything?" Scotty asked enthusiastically. "Just you and me?"

"What did you have in mind?" Johnny asked, curious, but reluctant to part with the family, much less Jenn, for *any* of what little time he had left.

"A good, long horseback ride. I can show you the ranch."

"That sounds nice, Scotty, but, uh—I was really hoping to spend some time with Jenn today. You and I have the rest of the summer to ride together. I only have a few days with your sister."

"Yeah," the young man said, obviously disappointed by Johnny's answer.

Johnny put a hand on the boy's shoulder. "I have an idea that might work for all of us, if you don't mind having your sister around."

Scotty grunted. "I always mind having my sister around."

Johnny laughed. "Spoken like a true brother." Then he paused, frowning slightly. "I envy you."

This time it was Scotty who reached out to Johnny, giving him a friendly slap on the back. "Hey, buddy, I forgot about that. I'm really sorry. And I'm just joking around about Jenn. She and I get along pretty well, all things considered. And I haven't seen her in a year. So not horses, then, I guess. What'd ya have in mind for us?"

"Not horses?" Johnny queried lightly.

"Naw. Not with my sister."

Johnny smiled at Scotty's continued use of drawled, slang speech. He knew the only thing the boy had ever wanted to be was a cowboy, and though Johnny knew perfectly well Scotty was educated enough to speak correct English, he found it amusing that the boy stuck to his guns—pun intended.

And Johnny could relate. He rather wished he could keep on with the humble, carefree life of a cowboy forever, but he knew it couldn't last.

Not forever. Not even close.

Hopefully, for at least these two weeks, and if God was merciful to him, the rest of the summer.

"I don't see why we still couldn't take that horseback ride you mentioned. I wondered if I could just invite Jenn to go along with us?"

Scotty belted out a laugh, looking utterly relieved. "You can ask, old man, but she ain't about to go with you...us."

"And why is that?" Johnny cocked a questioning brow at his friend.

"Because, big guy, your Jenn is deathly afraid of horses. I thought she would have told you that in one of your *'conversations.'*"

Johnny ignored the boy's teasing, preferring to go straight to the point. "She grew up on a ranch. How could she be afraid of horses?"

Scotty rolled to his stomach and cupped his chin in his palms. "I dunno if I should be telling you this or not. Maybe you should ask Jenn. But I always wondered if that was what sent her flying into the big city as fast as her wings would flap."

"What did?" Johnny asked, his patience wearing thin. He knew exactly what kind of response he'd get if he tried to ask Jenn anything remotely personal, yet he was determined to find out more about her, even if he had to wring it from her younger brother's neck.

"She never liked living on a ranch," Scotty said, now rolling onto his back and lacing his hands behind his head and staring straight up at the sky.

"I got that much," Johnny said dryly. "Now tell me what I don't know."

Scotty chuckled. "Testy. You must really like my sister a lot."

Johnny didn't want to think about that statement, so he continued to press the boy for details. "Just tell me what happened to her, Scotty, and spare me the lectures on the state of my heart."

Scotty laughed again. "Did I say anything about your heart?"

"Scotty," Johnny warned.

"All right, already." Scotty chuckled and pulled in a deep breath. "Jenn was about, I don't know, five or six when she got her first horse. 'Course, I wasn't born yet, so I've only heard the story secondhand, but it's one of those stories the family passes around."

He winked at Johnny. "Anyway, she'd been on horses before plenty of times, bein' that we lived on a ranch and all, but this horse was all hers, a birthday present from our folks."

Johnny didn't say a word to interrupt, now that Scotty was speaking freely.

"I think she must've been too excited or something. My folks knew how to pick good horseflesh, and they chose a real gentle gelding for her, a horse that had been around the block a few times, you know?"

"Mmm-hmm," Johnny answered.

"But Jenn was just a kid—an excited little girl with her very own horse. She'd been riding around the corral for several minutes when the gelding suddenly spooked and started rearing like a buckin' bronc. No one really knows why, even to this day. He dumped her but good, right into the corral fence. If I recall the story right, she broke a wrist and sprained both her ankles, but it wasn't really serious."

"Then what?" Johnny asked. "You aren't a real horseman until you've taken your first digger. Surely your parents knew to get her up and back on that horse riding as soon as possible."

"Oh, they tried, believe me. Still do, sometimes. But Jenn would scream like a banshee every time they tried to get her near a horse. After a while, my parents stopped trying to force the issue, though, like I said, they still offer to take her out on a horse every year when we're up here for the reunion."

"And every year she refuses."

"Exactly. Now you might be able to charm Jenn into a few moonlight kisses, but don't expect to be able to get her to ride with you."

The part about the moonlight kisses had Johnny's mind going in all kinds of directions for a few seconds, but he reeled his thoughts in—reluctantly.

"Be that as it may, I'm still gonna try," he said, standing to his full height and stretching to take the kinks out of his muscles.

"Brave man," Scotty said with a wink.

Stupid man, probably, Johnny thought, though he didn't say it aloud. Still, he couldn't shake the feeling that he needed to ask.

This was something he could help her with. The woman was still a complete enigma to him, but he'd seen the fear in her eyes. Maybe this whole horse thing had her rattled, being on the ranch and all.

He could help with that. He knew he could.

If she'd let him.

"So what's keeping you?" Scotty teased.

Johnny gave him his best frown, and then grinned widely. "You're lying on my bedroll."

Johnny couldn't find Jenn anywhere. The ranch house was sprawling, but it wasn't that big. He'd walked around it twice, crossing paths with nearly every member of the family along the way, some more than once. He thought about asking someone if they would be able to point him to where Jenn might be, but he knew enough about her now to know that, if she wanted her privacy, she wasn't going to announce her whereabouts to everyone.

He'd just about decided she must be out on the grounds somewhere, when he saw the slightest brush of the curtain next to the windowed alcove in the sitting room. On a hunch, he crept up to it, trying to keep his cowboy boots from clunking on the hardwood floor.

"Jenn?" he said softly, before brushing back the curtain with the back of his hand, not wanting to startle her by his sudden appearance.

He'd expected to find her reading, or just taking a few minutes of quiet time away from the hustle and bustle of her family, to bask in the sunshine like a lazy cat.

What he actually encountered when he pulled aside the curtain shocked him to the core, causing his breath to freeze in his lungs.

Jenn's blue eyes were huge as she met his gaze, and an expression of guilt and panic crossed her face as she instinctively skittered away from him into the far corner of the alcove. In the same moment, she quickly tried to pull the sleeve of her shirt down over her arm and hide a tube of antiscar liniment behind her back so Johnny couldn't see.

But he did.

Jenn knew she was too late, that her movements hadn't been quick enough for Johnny's keen gaze.

Johnny's eyes turned to a deep, forbidding shade of black as he slid in beside her and placed his hat on the seat next to him.

"Jenn," was all he said, as he took her wrist in one hand and carefully rolled up her sleeve with the other, baring her forearm. His touch was gentle and his gaze tender and understanding. His Adam's apple bobbed as if he were trying to speak, or swallow, but appeared to be able to do neither.

Which was why, if she could have, Jenn would have run as far and as fast as she could away from the man. Blockaded herself in her room and never come out.

But Johnny was holding her wrist like a vise. She couldn't move, but neither could she sit there and envelope the warmth of the sympathy in his gaze.

Not Johnny. Please, not him.

She'd thought she was alone, that no one would bother her. All she'd been doing was rubbing some scar-reducing cream onto her forearm, something she did several times a day when no one was looking.

Or at least when she *thought* no one was looking. This time she'd been caught.

And of all people, by Johnny Barnes.

She couldn't imagine anything worse. Except maybe the tears that sprang to her eyes. She would have dashed them away, except that she felt completely paralyzed by Johnny's presence.

"Jenn?" he asked softly, brushing his fingers along the scars on her arms.

She wished he would stop repeating her name and just come out and say what he was thinking. Actually, she wished he wasn't here at all.

"Just go away, Johnny, and leave me alone."

"No."

That one word stopped her cold. It wasn't harsh or condemning, which made it all the worse. Uttered gently and with that soft-spoken voice she couldn't resist, she looked everywhere but at him, or at her arm.

"Did you get these injuries from falling off the horse?" he asked, in the same mild tone. "No wonder you won't go near the animals."

"What?" She hadn't planned to talk to him at all, and she waited until he eased up on her wrist and she could pull away and make a dignified exit, or at least as much as she was able in her current state of mind. But his words confused her.

"When you fell into the fence," he explained gently. "Scotty said it was a corral. I just assumed it was a wooden fence. Was it barbed wire? Did your arm get tangled up when the horse threw you?"

Jenn still had no idea what he was talking about, and neither did Johnny, apparently. She scrambled to fill in the missing blanks, so she could answer him without giving anything away.

Horses?

Barbed wire?

Her mind flashed through a number of scenarios, but she still came up blank.

"I looked all over for you this morning. I wanted to ask you to take a ride with me tomorrow—on horseback. Scotty warned me you wouldn't want to go. Now I think I know why."

Jenn breathed an internal sigh of relief. Finally, she understood what he was talking about—when she'd been thrown from her horse as a youngster. Falling off horses she could deal with.

Not so much the truth.

And he'd brought it up, after all. She didn't have to say a thing, didn't have to invent a single falsehood. She could let him think whatever he wanted to, and have him be none the wiser as to the real source of her scars.

But it still felt like a lie, and Jenn had it up to her ears with lies. On one hand, adding this to her already enormous heap of fabrications seemed like such a small thing, especially considering the circumstances. If there was ever a reason to hide the truth, this was it.

Johnny dropped his free arm behind her, not quite touching her, but close enough to make her feel warm and cherished, as if he were hugging her close. She closed her eyes, savoring the feeling, if just for now.

She was an idiot, she realized. She knew she wasn't going to get out of this situation without some damage to her heart, but at the moment, she didn't care. The only thing that mattered was that Johnny *did* care.

And he wasn't anything like other men.

She felt the brush of his fingers against her cheek, and she leaned into them, savoring the rough calluses of this cowboy's work-worn hand.

"You've really been hurt, haven't you?"

His words made her freeze both inside and outside. Was he still talking about horses?

Part of her hoped so, and she wanted to let it go at that, or at least, she knew she should.

Yet there was a part of her, in the deepest recesses of her soul, which cried out to be released. She'd carried her secrets around so long, the ache had become a part of who she was, an integral part of her being. Her scars went far deeper than the flesh wounds she'd been tending, and she'd never told a single soul about either type of injury—inside or outside.

Until now.

She opened her eyes and met Johnny's gaze. His full, bow-shaped lips were pressed together as if he were experiencing pain of his own, merely by empathizing with hers. She saw it in his eyes, as well, so full of warmth and compassion.

He cared.

And he'd be gone in a week.

Suddenly, it didn't seem so far-fetched to share the real story with this man. It was a burden she'd carried around far too long. From what she knew of Johnny Barnes, he wouldn't judge, and he most certainly wouldn't tell anyone.

He couldn't.

Hot tears sprang once more to her eyes, as the pain and agony she'd kept bottled up for years rushed to the surface. She didn't even try to wipe away the moisture, knowing many more tears would be shed before she could say what she wanted to—*had* to say.

"These scars aren't from getting thrown from a horse, Johnny," she said, her voice twisted and scratchy. "I— I fell through a bay window."

"You did *what?*" Johnny asked, disbelief and fury warring on his face. "How?"

Her silence must have been answer enough, for he continued. "Who did this to you, Jenn? I'm going to take that man and—"

Jenn cut him off. "That wouldn't change my past, Johnny. Or my future."

His gaze, so focused on her own, was piercing her straight to the heart. His lips worked, but no sound came out for several seconds. Finally he whispered a coarse, "What?"

"This is going to be really hard to explain. I'm not sure I really understand all the implications myself. Some social worker I am, huh? I can't even handle my own problems."

"Who did this to you?" Johnny repeated, sounding as angry as Jenn had ever heard him. She wondered if he was angry at her. For hiding the truth. For being stupid enough to have put herself in the position of being thrown out of a window in the first place.

Jenn was angry enough at herself. She didn't need Johnny's censure. But she could hardly blame him. It was a shocking story.

"The scars are a constant reminder of what was. Is," she said, correcting herself. "The pain—the emotional pain—never really goes away."

"What happened?" Johnny asked again.

Jenn shook her head. "I think it's best if I start at the beginning."

Johnny nodded and gave her shoulders a comforting squeeze.

She took a deep breath and plunged in before she lost her nerve. "I never liked living on a ranch," she explained. "Not even as a small child. Maybe it was the whole getting-thrown-from-a-horse thing, I don't know. I just know I wanted out, and the older I got, the closer I was to graduating high school, the more I hated it."

She brushed at her tears with the palms of her hands. "The long and short of it is, by the time I was sixteen, I rebelled against everything good I'd been taught by my family."

"All teenagers rebel." Johnny sounded almost as if he were making excuses for her, but Jenn knew the truth: there was no excuse for her actions back then.

Or now, for that matter.

"Yeah? Well, not like I did. I was raised by a loving Christian family, and I knew better. I'd been taught well, but I didn't care to be anything like them. I couldn't see past the nose on my face, if you'll pardon the expression.

"Like most teenagers, I thought I knew everything. So I did anything I could to prove what a smart grown-up I was. Everything I'd been taught better than to do. I drank, I smoked and I ran with a bad crowd."

"I still don't understand," he said gently. "Lots of kids do that. But most people don't get thrown through a window." His fingers were soft as he traced the scars on her arm. "Don't tell me you got into a bar fight, like in the movies."

Johnny's light, teasing tone made it easier for her to face the truth. Jenn closed her eyes to shut out the painful memories, but they were coming fast and furious, and she opened her eyes again, finding more comfort in the strength of Johnny's gaze than in the darkness, the self-imposed, agonizing isolation she'd lived with all these years.

"There was this guy I really liked. He was quite a bit older than me—ten years. He was twenty-six years old, and I was sixteen. I was so flattered that he paid attention to me, that I didn't see the warning signs. I'm not even sure I knew what they were back then. Or else I was ignoring them."

"Warning signs?" Johnny asked gently.

Jenn shrugged. "I was always attracted to the bad boy image, and this guy had it in spades. It didn't occur to me that it was more than just an image, that the clothes he wore were an indication of what he was like inside his heart. He—I—"

She paused, regrouping. "At first he doted on me. He drove a Mustang and would give me rides home from school. He brought me presents. I'd been with him for weeks before he started slapping me around." She looked away from Johnny, her face reddening. "I was young enough and stupid enough to think he really cared for me, even when he hit me. He always apologized afterward, always told me how much he loved me."

Johnny's eyes turned a dark black and were filled with a look Jenn had never seen before. She rushed on, afraid to stop.

"You can probably guess the rest. Duke—his name was actually Darryl Duke, but everyone just called him Duke—took me back to his house one night. He was angry and drunk, but I didn't see it then. Here I was, thinking how mature I was, how special it was that Duke noticed me at all.

"He offered me a drink. When he came on to me, I didn't know what to do. I might have been rebellious, but I was a good girl at heart, and he scared me."

"He didn't take no for an answer."

"He was so nice at first, flattering me with romantic words. But when I started balking, he changed. He called me all sorts of names. Said I had led him on."

"Oh, Jenn."

"When he grabbed me, I struggled. I tried to get away from him. That's when he backhanded me hard across the face. The force of the blow set me off balance. I twisted in the air and realized too late I was going to…" Her sentence drifted off into the thick air.

"You don't have to say it, Jenn," Johnny said softly. "He knocked you through that window."

"I was so young, so stupid. I've asked myself over and over again why I got in that car. And I was so scared someone would find out, my family especially, that I didn't say a word to anyone."

"But you must have been badly hurt, to have scars like that," Johnny pointed out, gently tracing the lines on her arm. "You didn't go to the hospital?"

"No. That's why the scars are so bad. I think I must have instinctively held my arms over my face when I fell, because they got the brunt of the glass. But I didn't dare seek medical help. A doctor would have been obligated to call my parents."

"So, what did you do?"

"Went to a friend's house. She pulled out all the shards of glass left in my arms and bandaged me up. I've kept my arms hidden ever since."

"Which is why you wore long sleeves to the beach…why you didn't swim with the rest of your family."

"Yes."

Johnny snorted and shook his head. "And I thought you just didn't like to swim. I'm so sorry, Jenn. I'm as thickheaded as they come."

"Don't apologize," Jenn said, astounded that he would even suggest he was to blame for anything. "This is a secret I've kept for a long time. I wouldn't have expected you—or anyone—to guess the real reasons behind my actions. Please don't take that on yourself. It's my fault and my fault alone."

"It wasn't your fault." Johnny's voice was no longer soft-spoken, but as deep and hard as she'd ever heard it.

Jenn brushed at the tears on her cheeks. "I know," she said, and a wave of relief engulfed her so fiercely she began shaking. She *had* known she wasn't to blame, yet, until she'd said the words aloud, she had never— she realized with a flaming burst of insight—really forgiven herself.

She chuckled dryly. "I'm a trained social worker, remember? But knowing the truth and believing it are two different things."

"I wish there was something I could say, but there isn't," Johnny said, his soft voice back.

"I know. I don't expect anything from you, Johnny, except for you to keep your mouth shut."

Johnny nodded immediately. "Done."

Johnny wondered at the wisdom of the promise he made her, but he knew in his heart that, no matter how much he wanted to let her family know, to have them help and support her through the trauma she'd carried for so long, it was Jenn's decision to make.

And it was a decision she'd made long ago. That she'd confided in him filled him with a guilt-ridden sense of pride. He wanted to be there for her and was glad he was, but so many questions lingered.

Why him?

Why now?

And what could he do to help? He still didn't understand, and had the deepest feeling that he didn't know half of the story.

"I understand why you didn't say anything at the time," he said gently, again tracing the uneven, ragged edges that marked her forearm. "But why have you never told your family? I'm sure they would understand. And then you wouldn't have to hide anymore."

"It has been years, but it may as well have been yesterday. The wounds are so fresh. I have so much rage, guilt, fear. Deep, gut-wrenching emotions I can't even put a name to. At one point I even wanted to take my own life, though my folks put enough of the fear of God in me that I was too chicken to take the permanent way out, no matter how bad things were."

Johnny frowned. "Okay," he said, blowing out a breath. "You asked me to keep your secret, and I will. You can trust me, Jenn."

Jenn squeezed her eyes closed. "I know," she whispered raggedly.

"You are still in so much pain." Johnny didn't mean it as a question, and he didn't state it that way.

"Sometimes. Most of the time I just shove it down so far inside me I can hardly feel it. I've lived with it so long, it's only a dull ache now. Most of the time I hardly notice. It seems worse when I'm here at home, for some reason."

"I can only imagine," he said softly.

He would have said more, but suddenly he heard footsteps approaching the alcove.

Johnny didn't have time to think. All he knew was that Jenn's arms—her scars—were exposed. The secret she'd kept from her family for years.

He did the first thing that came to mind, something he knew would distract Jenn's family long enough for her to cover up.

He threw himself in front of her, framed her face with his hands, and kissed her.

Jenn's heart had leapt clear out of her chest when she'd heard footsteps. And then, before she had the chance to so much as even take a breath, Johnny was kissing her.

Her head swam, her senses overwhelmed by the tender way he framed her face with his large, callused hands. By the soft, gentle warmth of his lips on hers.

One week ago she would have slapped any man who would have come anywhere close to kissing her. Now, she leaned into the kiss, wanting to forget everything but the comfort Johnny offered.

Dimly, she heard the curtain open, and Granny and Auntie Myra call out, "Gotcha!" She didn't even care if her family was watching.

Then she felt Johnny nudge her arm with his elbow and immediately realized his true intent. He was blocking Granny's and Auntie Myra's view, so she could cover up her arm before they saw the scars.

So she could keep her secret.

Bless the man. Even if it was next to impossible to think rationally enough to roll down her sleeve with Johnny kissing her that way.

And he just kept on kissing her.

She didn't fight him.

Just the opposite, in fact. She leaned into his kiss, wrapping one arm around his neck and threading her fingers into the soft, curly hair at the nape of his neck.

It wasn't that she'd never been kissed before. She'd kissed more than her share of young, inexperienced boys—part of the reason, maybe, why she'd been drawn to Duke, who, at twenty-six years old, had appeared so different to her—better: a man. Not a boy.

At least, until she'd met up with Duke's cruelty. Since the brutal encounter which had made her distrust, even hate, men in general, she'd been a card-carrying member of the Never Been Kissed Club.

Didn't want it.

Didn't need it.

Just leave me alone, thank you very much, Jenn had thought.

Now she realized what she'd been missing. Johnny was a man, not a gangly teenage boy. And he was as kind and tender as Duke had been cruel.

There was no denying it anymore, no matter how she told herself differently. She was experiencing undeniable, flag-waving feelings for Johnny.

"Hello-o-o," Granny hooted with an earsplitting chuckle. "Take a breath, for mercy's sake, before you both pass out!"

Johnny broke off the kiss with a laugh. "If you insist," he said, casually turning toward Jenn's relatives, his arm still firm around her shoulders. "Though I've got to say, kissing your granddaughter is a good site more interesting than bantering with you two."

Auntie Myra clutched a hand to her chest, over her heart, staggering dramatically. "You wound us, Johnny," she teased. "And look at Jenn's face. She's as red as a ripe tomato."

Jenn knew that much was true. She'd felt the blood

rush to her face the moment Johnny had drawn away. His arm was still around her, but she felt as if she'd lost something very valuable, and she desperately wanted it back. She wondered vaguely if kissing Johnny would be like that every time, or if it had only been the circumstances.

So much for no public displays of affection. What would her family be expecting of them, now that they had seen what looked like stolen kisses?

What did *she* expect?

She couldn't answer that question, especially not with Johnny so near. She stood quickly and turned to Johnny, brushing her thumb across his scratchy cheek. "Thank you," she said for his ears only. "I owe you one."

He reached an arm around her neck and pulled her closer, brushing a soft kiss against her cheek before whispering, "You don't owe me a thing, darlin'."

Chapter Eight

Johnny slept under the stars once again. He could hardly sit through supper, with all the smothered grins and speculative glances Jenn's family was laying on the two of them. He had a good notion to slam his palms against the table and tell them to just knock it off, that Jenn had already been through more in one day than any woman should have to bear, not to mention the constant agony of the past she'd confided in him.

But in the end, Johnny remained silent. For one thing, her family was just being…well, her family. Laughing, teasing and joking all the time. They loved one another and meant no harm.

Even so, Johnny had reached for Jenn's hand underneath the table when it was time to say grace.

She'd pulled her hand away.

And why wouldn't she? The true source of her embarrassment and pain today was *him*.

After all she'd revealed to him in confidence, all the fear and loathing he'd seen in her eyes when she men-

tioned her past, he'd gone right ahead and done the stu-
pidest, most hurtful thing he could possibly have done
under the circumstances.

He had kissed her.

He could justify his reasons until the end of his days,
but the truth was, he was no better than Duke, the man
Jenn so abhorred.

Johnny had taken advantage of Jenn in a weak moment, and he knew it.

Never mind that it was the only solution he could
think of in such a short and supercharged moment. No
matter that his action had been to save Jenn, to keep her
scars from her family's notice. What had started out as
another one of his unprecedented gallant moves had
turned into something else entirely.

He could have—*should* have—let her go the moment
she'd tugged her shirtsleeve back down to hide her scars.
Instead, he'd allowed the moment to linger. Truth be
told, he'd wanted that kiss to go on forever.

But throwing himself so wholeheartedly at a woman
so clearly—and rightly—gun-shy of men, well, that
was just plain stupid.

Stupid.

The act was done, and he couldn't take it back. But
there was something he could do.

He'd make sure it didn't happen again.

Even if his own heart was shattered in the process.

Jenn was up early the next morning. The sun shined
brightly through the windows and there wasn't a cloud
in the sky.

It was a good day to learn to ride a horse.

She didn't know exactly when in the night she'd made that decision, but by morning her mind was made up. Johnny had reached out to her with an offer to help conquer her fear of horses.

He was already well on his way to helping her conquer her fear of men.

She'd been living in fear too long, she realized as she laced up her running shoes, not having a pair of riding boots to don. Fear of the past had chained her future. As a social worker, she recognized this in others, but she'd never seen it in herself.

It had, she realized with a secret smile, taken a humble cowboy to do that for her.

She was beginning to think—*hope, really*—that this charade she and Johnny had started might actually have turned into something real. Something valuable, that would last far beyond these two precious weeks.

Never in a million years would she have imagined herself falling for a cowboy, but there it was, in black and white.

At least she thought so, until she entered the dining room for breakfast. Johnny and Scotty were speaking in low tones when she arrived. Johnny took one quick glance at her and then looked away, a frown creasing his brow as he stared down at his breakfast plate.

Jenn had dressed with special care this morning in her skinny jeans and a soft pink cotton shirt. She'd spent extra time arranging her silky curls, though she knew they'd soon be hopelessly windblown on the Wyoming range.

The least the man could do was appreciate her efforts, but he wouldn't even look at her. She stared at him, trying to force his gaze upon her, but he stubbornly refused to glance her way.

It was Scotty who finally said something to break the awkward silence. "We're goin' riding, sis, not to a fashion show," he teased.

Jenn supposed that was her brother's gangly way of a backhanded compliment, but she glared at him anyway, just for good measure.

Johnny looked up then, but not directly at her, shoving his fingers through his thick black curls.

"You're going *riding,* Jenn?" he queried, sounding astonished, though not at all the kind of surprise Jenn was hoping for.

He almost sounded as if he wasn't the one who'd asked her to come in the first place. She didn't know whether to be angry or hurt.

Jenn sat down at the side of the table opposite Johnny, clattering her dishes on the hard oak. Why did he not want her to go? What had happened to change his mind?

"I—I can see I'd just be in the way," she stammered. "I'll just—" She stood, unable to finish her sentence. She didn't want to be where she wasn't wanted, especially where Johnny was concerned.

Johnny reached across the table and gently but firmly grasped her hand to keep her from leaving. "No. I promised to teach you to ride, and I will."

"This I gotta see," Scotty quipped with glee. "Better than a circus."

Finally, Johnny met Jenn's gaze, but it was as if the sparkle, the light in his eyes Jenn had so grown to appreciate, had been smothered out. His gaze was hooded with shadow, his midnight-blue eyes appearing almost black. The adorable, amused quirk of his lips was gone, as well, and his jaw was clenched so tightly Jenn could see a muscle working there.

She was once again batting a thousand, Jenn thought. She had completely misread the situation from yesterday and now Johnny was acting like a cougar trapped on a bluff.

Jenn felt foolish. She had spent so many years running away from relationships, that the first time a man kissed her, she'd fallen right into his arms.

And why not? Johnny was handsome, charming, witty—and definitely *not* interested.

Jenn had known perfectly well why Johnny had thrown himself in front of her the way he had in the window nook yesterday, and why he'd kissed her. It was to help her keep her secret from her family, and nothing more.

She'd obviously misread any other emotion or intent on Johnny's part. Considering her self-imposed limited experience with the opposite gender, that insight shouldn't have surprised her.

But it did.

And it hurt.

Johnny stood and moved to the wall, where he took his hat off the peg and planted it on his head. "I'll go out and saddle you a horse, Jenn."

Jenn sat staring after him, her elbows on the table and her fingers clasped together, but did not immediately get up to leave.

Scotty looked from Jenn to the door Johnny had so abruptly exited, and then back again. "Did I miss something here?" he asked. For once, there wasn't a trace of brotherly teasing in his voice.

Jenn shook her head, thinking her brother's quiet concern was harder to deal with than if he'd simply made fun of her as he usually did. It wasn't that she didn't want to confide in Scotty about her feelings for Johnny as much as that she didn't know what she would say.

She didn't know *how* she felt.

"It's nothing," she said at last, feeling she had to say something, even if it sounded flat to her own sensitive ears.

"You guys have a lovers' spat?"

Jenn chuckled, but the sound was empty. "Believe me, Scotty, we most definitely did *not* have a 'lovers' spat,' as you put it."

How could they? She and Johnny didn't have a *lovers'* anything.

"He really likes you, you know." Scotty's usually loud, boisterous voice was barely more than a whisper, and even more surprisingly, her brother refused to look her in the eye.

Jenn perked up for just a moment, hope sparking to life at her brother's simple, direct words. "Did he tell you that?"

Scotty shook his head, then stood and reached for his own hat. "No. He didn't have to."

With that, her brother also exited. Jenn sat motionless, though she was shaking inside. Her mind felt like it was being pulled a billion ways at once, not to mention her heart and emotions.

She wished she'd never created this tangled web. She wished even more that Johnny hadn't played along. Most of all, she wished it wasn't a farce at all.

That the kiss had meant something—something real. As it had to her. But if Johnny's peculiar behavior this morning was anything to go by, all her wishes amounted to nothing.

With a sigh, Jenn stood and stretched. This was going to be a long enough day just trying to learn to ride a stupid horse, without having to think about her relationship, or rather lack of a relationship, with Johnny.

With effort, she shifted her thoughts to the ride to come. Her fear of horses was real enough to distract her, at least for the time being.

By the time she'd gathered sufficient courage to approach the corral, Johnny already had a dapple gray quarter horse gelding saddled, bridled and tied to the corral fence by a rope halter. Reluctantly, Jenn moved to Johnny's side, though she stayed on the opposite side of the fence from both the horse and the man.

"You can do this, Jenn," Johnny said, his voice so low she could barely make out the words.

"I think so," she replied, not completely truthfully. She wasn't sure she could find the courage to actually mount the horse, much less make any reasonable attempt to ride him.

But then again, she never thought she'd trust a man, either, and Johnny had worked through that barrier in the space of a week, merely by his patience and charm.

She only hoped that *charm* extended to horses, in particular the gray in front of her.

"This here's Silver," Johnny said, running his hand down the horse's neck and affectionately rubbing the tuft of mane between his ears.

"Oh, now that's an original name," Jenn quipped, glad to be thinking about something other than actually mounting up.

Johnny threw back his head and laughed. Jenn was glad to see the calm, steadfast gelding didn't shy away from the boisterous sound, or even appear particularly interested. Johnny truly had taken care to select a calm mount for her, for which she was especially thankful.

Johnny raised an eyebrow, and then winked slyly. "Come on over the fence, darlin'. You aren't going anywhere from there."

"Wasn't the Lone Ranger's horse white?" she asked, trying to continue that wayward train of thought even as she slipped through the space in the wooden fence—still a good two feet away from both horse and man.

Johnny had winked at her. And he'd called her darlin'. Maybe she'd overreacted to his behavior at breakfast. Now Johnny appeared nearly as calm and unruffled as the nickering horse he was urging her toward.

Johnny reached out a hand to her. "Come on over here, Jenn. You don't have to mount up until you're completely comfortable with Silver."

She didn't move, and he wiggled his fingers to indicate he was waiting for her.

"You have nothing to worry about," he said in a low, composed tone she was certain worked at least as well on her mount as it did on Jenn. "I'll be right here with you," he promised earnestly. "And as for this old gray, he's the calmest, gentlest horse you'll ever have the pleasure of riding."

Yeah, Jenn thought. *That's what they said last time, and look where it got me.*

Even so, she stepped forward slowly, tentatively reaching out to take Johnny's hand. The feel of his rough, callused palm in hers was oddly reassuring, despite her unrelenting reluctance to continue toward her waiting mount.

When she reached Johnny's side, he didn't speak. Neither did he try to force her to touch the gigantic beast. They just stood quietly, Johnny looking down at Jenn and Jenn eyeing the horse.

Johnny was every bit a man of his word, Jenn realized with relief. He wasn't going to push her in this. The cowboy could be so incredibly thoughtful sometimes, despite how gruff he'd been with her at breakfast.

Knowing Johnny was by her side gave her the courage she might otherwise have lacked. So, with a deep breath, she reached her hand out and brushed it along the gelding's neck as she'd seen Johnny do earlier.

The horse didn't flinch. Jenn wasn't sure if it was because of Silver's gentle nature or because of the way Johnny held the halter tightly in his grip, but whatever it was, it was working.

"Hello, Silver," she said in the voice she instinctively used with animals and small children. She had to smile when the horse nickered and leaned into her hand.

Johnny's reassuring smile helped, too. He spoke to the horse quietly while Jenn continued getting to know Silver, brushing her hand along his mane, his side, and eventually even down the blaze of his muzzle.

After a few moments getting to know the horse, Jenn dropped Johnny's hand and turned to him, looking him straight in the eye. "I'm ready," she said firmly, but refusing to look back at Silver.

"You sure?" Johnny asked gently. "You don't have to hurry this along, darlin'. Take all the time you want. I'm not in a hurry, and you shouldn't be, either."

"Look, Johnny. If you are going to get me on that beast's back, you'd better do it now, while I've still got the guts to try. Just tell me what I have to do."

She eyed the saddle horn and the stirrup on the side of the horse that was closest to her. The saddle horn she could reach if she stretched, but there was no way she could see herself getting a foot in the stirrup.

"I think I'm going to need a little help with this mounting business," she muttered, more to herself than to Johnny.

He chuckled softly. "Not a problem."

She expected Johnny to give her a foothold, but instead he simply grasped her by the waist and lifted her onto the saddle, with no strain on his part. The act left Jenn dizzy and a little out of breath, and not because she was six feet off the ground, on top of a shifting animal.

Once Johnny was sure she had her balance in the saddle, he moved back to once again firmly grasp the halter. He was positive Silver was a good match for her, but he didn't want to take any chances that the horse would start moving around.

"Feet in the stirrups," he instructed calmly. "Heels down. You want to balance with your knees, not with that death grip you have on the saddle horn."

Johnny winked at her to let her know he was teasing, and Jenn gave a nervous laugh. Even so, she straightened in the saddle and balanced herself with her legs.

"I'm going to slip the bridle reins over the saddle horn for right now, then lead Silver with the halter," he explained as he did just that. "Nice and slow. If you feel like you have to hold on to the saddle, do, but I want you to feel the rhythm of the horse. Try to move with him, not against him. We won't go any further until you can balance without holding on."

"Johnny, are you sure—" she started, as Johnny untied the halter from the fence.

He looked up at her, locking her gaze with his. "Do you trust me?" he asked softly.

"Yes," she immediately answered. "It's the horse I don't trust."

"I've got Silver well in hand. He's not going anywhere I don't tell him to. Now, I'm going to start leading him around the ring at a nice, slow walk. You just relax and enjoy the ride."

She made a soft, strangled sound in her throat, but Johnny kept his chuckle under his breath.

He started off in a slow circle, walking next to Silver's head and keeping his gaze on Jenn. Surprisingly, it wasn't long before her grip on the saddle horn loosened, and then fell entirely as she placed her palms on her thighs.

"I'm getting this!" she exclaimed, then clamped a hand over her mouth. "I can't help being excited, Johnny, and I think that's what got me into trouble last time. I'm afraid I'll freak Silver out and he'll balk like the last horse did."

"Any cowboy worth his salt gets excited when he's in the saddle. You think those rodeo guys aren't pumped with adrenaline? Horses can sense agitation, but it doesn't necessarily follow that your horse will freak out and you'll get thrown or anything."

"Those rodeo guys know how to stay on a horse at a dead run. I'm still not positive I can keep my balance at a walk."

"We can call it a day," Johnny suggested mildly. "If you want to, I mean." He was consciously baiting her, appealing to her stubborn streak.

Jenn frowned at him. "Look, cowboy, I came out here today to learn to ride, and that's exactly what I'm going to do."

Johnny tipped his hat at her. "An admirable quality, stubbornness."

Her frown turned to a smile. "Whatever works. What do I do next?"

"Slide the reins up off the saddle horn, but keep them loose." Jenn did as he said, but kept the reins extended so far down they were nearly slipping right off the horse's neck.

"Not that loose," Johnny said with a laugh. He reached up and adjusted the reins, threading them through her fingers in the old western style. "Now you can lead the horse on your own. It's like driving a car. Want Silver to go left, move your hand left. Right is right, stop is backward—gently."

"And go?"

She had loosened up while he'd been leading her around the corral, but now she looked as stiff as an ice sculpture. The poor woman really was terrified, but her determination was greater than her fear.

Johnny felt his own sense of determination rising. He wasn't going to let anything happen to Jenn. Not on his watch.

"Loosen up, darlin'. Your posture, not the reins. I'm not going to let old Silver bolt on you."

"You'd better not."

Johnny loosened the halter to where it had a couple of feet of lead on it, but he did not entirely release his hold on the rope. "I'm not letting go, see? Just nudge your heels lightly into Silver's side and he'll go."

Jenn's first few attempts at nudging were barely visible to Johnny's eye. He grinned. "A little harder than that, hon. The horse has to feel it."

Jenn squeezed her eyes shut and gave Silver a good prod with her heels. The horse moved off at the same slow walk he'd had when Johnny was leading him around. Jenn's eyes popped open and widened in surprise.

"Well, how about that?" she asked, sounding amazed. And pleased.

"Try a couple of turns," he suggested when she'd walked Silver around the corral a few times in a clockwise motion. "Now, halt."

Jenn was magnificent, Johnny thought. Not too many people would be able to face their fears with as much courage as this woman did. More to the point, if she kept this up, she would end up an excellent horsewoman. Too bad he wouldn't be around to see her triumph.

"I'm ready," Jenn announced, joy evident in her voice. "Let's do it, Johnny."

"Do what?" he asked. Her big blue eyes were sparkling with a new light that made Johnny's chest feel like it was going to explode.

"Go for a ride. That's what you asked me out here for, isn't it?"

"Yeah, but—"

"But nothing. Saddle up, cowboy, and let's ride the range."

His gaze locked with hers, intense and questioning. "You're sure about this?"

Jenn chuckled softly. She wasn't sure about anything. "No. But I'm going to do it anyhow."

Scotty sauntered from the house, walking to the corral fence and leaning his arms on it. "I've been watching from the window," he said, amazement in his voice. "I gotta hand it to ya, Johnny. I thought only God worked miracles."

Johnny frowned at him. "It wasn't a miracle. And it wasn't me. It was your sister. She's fantastic, isn't she?"

Scotty snorted loudly and made a face at the both of them.

"Johnny and I are going riding," Jenn announced, holding her chin high against the disbelief in her brother's expression. "Are you coming along, or not?"

Scotty looked from Jenn to Johnny and back, scratching the peach fuzz under his chin. Jenn held her breath, secretly hoping he would decline. While she loved her brother, she wanted this time alone with Johnny.

When Scotty raised an eyebrow at her, she knew her thoughts had been transparent on her face. "Uh, I don't think so," he said, snickering at Johnny's back as Johnny made his way to the stable to saddle his own mount. "Three's a crowd, and all that."

Jenn felt guilty about not including her brother. They'd never been close, with their age difference and all, but she loved him. "Come along. It's probably safer for me to ride with two seasoned cowboys than just one."

Scotty beamed at Jenn's compliment. "Naw. Really.

I promised to play chess with Granddad anyhow. You two go and have your fun."

Her brother turned and walked back to the house just as Johnny entered the corral, leading his own sturdy quarter horse, a large black mare which he'd brought with him in Scotty's horse trailer.

"He's not coming with us?" Johnny asked as he opened the corral gate.

"No," replied Jenn. "I believe he thought he might be infringing upon—well, a romantic rendezvous between you and me." She felt the blush rise on her cheeks and she looked away from Johnny.

He chuckled. "Scotty's loss. I guess I'll be the only one lucky enough to share your company."

Jenn thought back to their first meeting, when she'd so sternly demanded "no alone time" with this handsome cowboy. Now she couldn't wait to be alone with Johnny for an entire afternoon.

"We'll keep it at a slow walk, all right?" Johnny said, as he mounted up and led his horse outside the corral. "If you ever feel uncomfortable, just let me know. Remember, I'll be right by your side."

Funny, but she wasn't afraid. At least not of the horse. Her feelings for Johnny, maybe. And she wasn't the least sure she could rein those in with a simple backward tug.

Johnny held his horse until they were evenly paced. They rode for a while without talking, but Jenn didn't feel uncomfortable, either with the horse or with the man. There were no awkward gaps that made her need to fill the space with words. It was enough just to be out here with Johnny, riding side by side, enjoying the magnificent view of the ranch.

"Thank you," Jenn said softly a few minutes later.

"For what?" Johnny asked, his voice low and a little scratchy.

"You know perfectly well for what. For getting me up on this horse. I never realized how spectacular the landscape really is up here."

"Like what?"

"Well, for one thing, I thought it was all dead grass. I had no idea so many types of wildflowers grew on my grandparents' property."

"No?" he asked with a sideways glance at her. "Pull your mount to a halt for a moment, darlin'. Just hold steady there, okay?"

Jenn did as she was asked, wondering what was wrong. Had her cinch loosened, and she was sliding off her mount without even knowing about it?

Johnny slid off his horse and pulled the reins over the animal's neck, dropping them to the ground and leaving the horse free.

"Should you be doing that?" Jenn asked, wondering how they were going to get back to the ranch if Johnny's horse decided to take off on his own.

"Lucy here comes when I whistle," Johnny said with a laugh.

"Lucy? You named your horse Lucy?" It just didn't seem like the name a cowboy would give his horse. She shook her head and laughed.

"Yeah. Just fit her personality, I guess."

"I guess," Jenn repeated, still laughing.

Johnny started walking, looking around at the ground, as if he'd lost something.

"What are you looking for?" she asked, not so impatient as curious.

"Shh," he said, holding his index finger to his lips. "Just give me a second."

Jenn raised her eyebrows but said nothing.

"Here it is. I knew I'd find it if I looked close enough." His back was to her so she didn't see what he reached down and grabbed until he'd turned back toward her, a long-stemmed wildflower with dangling blue petals in his hand. "Bluebells," he said. "Or at least, that's what I call them. They remind me of your eyes."

Jenn choked up as he handed his heartfelt gift to her. No one had ever given her anything so thoughtful. The single wildflower held far more significance than the fancy roses she'd sent herself.

She tucked the precious flower into her hair, thinking she'd press it into a book when she arrived back at the ranch house. It was certainly a moment she didn't want to forget.

Ever.

"Thank you," she choked out belatedly, as Johnny remounted.

Johnny just shook his head and looked away from her. "Let's go that way," he said, pointing to the west. "Looks like some nice terrain."

Jenn turned her mount that direction, wanting to say more, but not knowing what to say or how to express what she was feeling.

She wasn't even sure *what* she was feeling, only that her emotions were in such a jumble, she was surprised they didn't cause her to fall right off her horse.

She was about to say thank you again, she realized,

but Johnny had already blown off her gratitude twice. She was relatively certain, she thought with a soft smile, that he wouldn't want to hear it a third time.

She was still pondering what she *should* say when she suddenly heard a sound she'd been taught to recognize from childhood and which she had been afraid of all her life.

The chilling rattle of a snake.

Chapter Nine

Jenn didn't have a second's time to consider what that might mean to her or her mount, before Silver bucked sideways and bolted at a dead run. The horse's sudden jerk back should have thrown her, but she'd been concentrating carefully on riding just the way Johnny had taught her, and somehow, some way, she'd remained in the saddle despite the horse's lurch.

But she had only ridden at a slow walk. Now the horse was galloping at a speed so fast the countryside was flying by her in a blur. Instinctively, she leaned forward, desperately gripping the saddle horn and the horse's mane for dear life with her hands, while trying to remember what Johnny had taught her about using her legs and heels to keep the horse under her. She still held the reins in her left hand, along with the saddle horn, but only because they'd been laced through her fingers by Johnny.

Now she knew why.

At first, her concentration was solely on staying in the

saddle and keeping her stomach from lurching, both from the fear of losing her seat and the feeling that the earth was coming up to meet her with each stride of the horse.

She could hear Johnny calling to her in the distance. "Pull up, Jenn. Pull up on the reins!"

Except, she couldn't pull up on the reins, or otherwise steer the careening beast, because she knew if she let go of the saddle horn, even for a brief moment, her ride would be over.

Her *life* might be over. No telling what a fall from a horse going this speed might do to her—and that was if she didn't hit her head on a rock when she fell.

No, she was going to have to continue holding on for dear life, and hope that eventually the horse would tire and stop on its own.

It was then she realized just where Silver was headed. She didn't know the ranch as well as the rest of her family, but if she wasn't mistaken, there was a steep ravine ahead, with a drop of at least twelve feet or more. There was no way she'd survive if the horse went over the edge, and she was helpless to stop him.

She closed her eyes, gritting her teeth against the inevitable. Either she would have to jump from the horse or she would hit the ravine.

Neither option looked good.

It was as if time slowed down, though the clatter of hoofbeats never ceased.

She was going to die. And she hadn't even made peace with herself, let alone God, not that she believed in God. But her life was suddenly over, and what did she have to show for it?

And what did it mean—*really* mean—to die?

A giant nothingness?

Would she simply cease to exist?

Her soul cried out against that thought. How could she *be,* and then suddenly *not be?*

And still the horse continued on at a gallop, headed straight for the ravine. Jenn was barely aware she was screaming, no longer caring if Silver might be affected by her own terror. The situation had gone far beyond that now, and the ravine was closing in on her.

She could still hear Johnny yelling but could no longer make out his words. She was beginning to feel dizzy, with the world whirling around her. Maybe she would pass out entirely.

Maybe it was better that way.

And then Johnny was in front of her, just at the edge of the ravine, his horse rearing up and Johnny, hat in hand, waving his arms and yelling for all he was worth.

It took Jenn a moment to realize what he was doing, and even longer still to recognize that his plan had worked. He'd risked his own life for hers, putting himself and his own horse directly in the path of the ravine, forcing Silver to divert to the side, to safety.

It worked, and Silver, frothy and snorting from the run, quickly slowed and began sidestepping in his agitation. Jenn didn't let go of the horse or the saddle, but she turned her head to see Johnny still on the edge of the cliff.

He appeared to be having trouble controlling his own mount, though Jenn struggled to understand how that could be, consummate horseman that Johnny was. He held a good seat despite Lucy slip-sliding on the loose gravel near the edge of the ravine. Johnny appeared to be helping her, guiding her away from the danger.

Then his horse lost her footing and half reared to avoid the deep, deathly fall into the ravine.

Lucy recovered and quickly skittered away to safety. Johnny was not so lucky.

Jenn slid off her now still mount, screaming in terror as Johnny was heaved off the saddle, his hands grasping desperately at the air as he plunged down the side of the ravine.

Jenn hit the dirt at a dead run, not caring when she slid on the gravel and had to right herself with her palms, not even noticing they were bleeding from the small, sharp rocks.

She slowed only as she reached the edge of the ravine, dropping to her stomach to look over its edge. Johnny's body lay unmoving at the bottom, his neck cocked at an odd angle.

Had he hit his head on a rock? There were certainly enough ominous-looking stones down there, many around Johnny's still body.

"Johnny!" she called, over and over, but he didn't respond.

He obviously couldn't, Jenn thought.

He was dead. And she'd killed him.

She scrambled down the ravine, ignoring the sound of tearing cloth, as thorny branches reached out to scratch her skin raw. "Johnny. Oh, God, please don't let Johnny be dead."

She didn't even realize she was praying.

It was only when she knelt before Johnny's body that she realized his chest was rising and falling. Relief flooded through her, followed quickly by terror. Johnny was alive, but he was unconscious, which meant he'd suffered a good knock to the head. She could now see his head had, in fact, landed on a sizeable stone.

What should she do now?

For all she knew, every bone in his body could be broken. And she was out in the middle of nowhere, with nothing and nobody but the horses, presumably still on the ridge above her. She reached for the cell phone she always carried with her. It was a lost cause. There was no service this far out in the middle of nowhere. With an audible growl of frustration, she jammed the phone back into her pocket.

Think, she commanded herself.

Okay. First aid. She could administer some sort of help to Johnny. She'd taken courses in first aid from the community shelters where she worked. Mostly what she remembered, though, was CPR, and that wasn't going to help her now.

Johnny's heart was beating, and he was breathing, albeit shallowly. What was the correct course of action for a bump on the noggin?

Concentrate.

Johnny's face was becoming paler by the moment. Beads of sweat had formed on his forehead.

Was he going into shock?

Quickly, Jenn unbuttoned her long-sleeved shirt, glad she'd worn a T-shirt underneath for the ride today. She rolled her shirt into a makeshift pillow and slid it as gently as possible under Johnny's head, trying not to move his neck any more than she had to.

She found a medium-size rock which had a flat edge, and put it underneath his feet to raise them slightly.

A blanket. She needed a blanket. The sun was roasting down on them, but a shock victim might not feel the heat, and even so, she knew she needed to cover him.

And water. He needed water.

Jenn knew both items were tied to her saddle, so she quickly scrambled back up the ravine's steep incline, hoping she'd find her horse, or Johnny's, when she made it to the top.

Both horses were grazing just east of the ravine, looking for all the world as if nothing had happened. Her horse didn't even spook as she approached. Silver let her get what she needed from the saddle without bothering so much as to stop nibbling at the grass.

She only wished Johnny could recover as quickly from the trauma of the past few minutes. If he didn't... Well, she wasn't going to let herself go there now.

She needed to stay alert. Focused.

Positive.

With the needed supplies tucked under one arm, Jenn slid back down the ravine to Johnny's side. Murmuring light, comforting words under her breath, she quickly covered him up with the scratchy wool blanket and then splashed her handkerchief with some of the cool water from her canteen.

"Come on, Johnny, don't do this to me," she whispered as she gently dabbed the fabric against his brow. "You can't leave me now. I just found you."

She was putting a second splash of water on the handkerchief when Johnny groaned.

"Oh, my head." He lifted an arm toward his forehead, but Jenn stopped him.

"Shh. Don't try to move, Johnny. You fell down the ravine. You've been hurt."

To her surprise, Johnny chuckled, if weakly. "Yeah, that much I got."

Lying on death's door and still cracking jokes. Or maybe she was being overdramatic. Maybe his injuries looked worse than they were.

There was only one way to know for sure.

"I don't want you to move. Not a muscle, do you hear me, cowboy?"

"Uh," he answered, his eyes flitting open for just a moment before he closed them again. "Don't think I could if I wanted to."

"I've got to ride back to the ranch and get help," she stated as calmly as possible, though her heart was racing on the inside. There was no use making Johnny panic by her going into hysterics, so she pushed her apprehension to the back of her mind.

"Uh-huh," he answered in a quiet, scratchy tone. "I'm not going anywhere." He sounded as if he weren't quite all together, and Jenn's heart clenched. Maybe the head injury was worse than she thought.

"I'll be back as quick as I can. In the meantime, you just lie still. I *will* be back," she promised him fervently, laying a gentle hand on his forearm for emphasis. "It won't take nearly as long to return for you in a four-wheel drive."

Johnny lay unmoving, and Jenn thought he'd passed out again. She laid her hand on his chest, over his heart. "I'm praying for you, Johnny."

She didn't know where the words had come from. Maybe from being around her family too long. Maybe from the lack of having anything else to say.

He couldn't hear her anyway.

She was about to rise when Johnny's hand snaked out and grabbed her wrist. Startled, she tried to pull away, but even in his weakened state, Johnny was stronger than she was.

She felt one moment of panic, the sheer terror her experience with Duke had branded into her.

But this was different. This was Johnny. And he wasn't hurting her, on the off chance he was truly capable of doing so in his present condition.

He just wasn't letting go.

"Are you really? Are you really, Jenn?" he rasped through a dry throat.

Jenn took a moment to dribble some water from the canteen down his throat before she answered.

"Really what?"

"Really praying."

"I guess so. I don't know." She paused and shook her head. "Why are you asking me this?"

She should be racing for help, but Johnny wouldn't let her go. His eyes had reopened and his midnight-blue gaze was clear, holding her every bit as firmly as his grip on her wrist.

"I pray with my eyes open, Jenn," he said in a coarse whisper.

Jenn had no idea what that statement meant. Maybe the man was delirious, though his eyes were clear and piercing straight through to her soul.

"Look, cowboy, you're going to be in a world of hurt if I don't get back to the ranch and get you some help."

"Yeah," he agreed, dropping her wrist and covering his ribs protectively. "It hurts, all right."

"Don't move," she warned him again, pressing the

canteen into his hand. "Not a muscle, Johnny. I'll be back as soon as I can."

She didn't wait to see his response, but rather hiked up the ravine wall as fast as she could, ignoring the sharp pain in her ankles when her feet slid on the treacherous gravel.

One thing at a time now. Ravine. Horse. Ranch.

Horse.

Great. She'd made a lot of progress today, but she wasn't even remotely over her fear of horses, and now she was alone with a great, big giant of a horse, and without Johnny to help guide her.

Or to assist her in mounting.

She approached Silver and took up his reins, glad when the horse didn't balk at her presence. Surely, he must sense her fear of horses, not to mention the apprehension she was feeling at Johnny's precarious condition, but he remained calm.

Why had Johnny given her such a gigantic animal to ride? How was she supposed to get into the saddle? Johnny had lifted her onto it before.

But she had to get in that saddle. One way or another.

Now.

She knotted the reins and slid them over the saddle horn, which was right about level with her forehead. This was not going to be easy.

You've seen this done a thousand times, she coached herself. Everyone in her family rode horses all the time—and they didn't need handsome cowboys hoisting them into the saddle. Just like on television, the members of her family made it look easy to swing up on top of their horses. Jenn had the sinking feeling it wasn't as easy as it looked in the movies.

Standing to the left of the horse and as close as possible, she raised her leg, trying to get a foothold in the stirrup. If she could just get one foot in, maybe she could boost herself up by the saddle horn.

This was one time when being short was definitely not an advantage. Her foot didn't even come close to the stirrup, no matter how she twisted, turned or hopped.

There had to be another way. She looked around for something big enough to stand on—a boulder maybe, or a tree stump. But there was nothing in sight.

Her heart continued at its frantic pace, and Jenn felt as if it might burst right out of her chest if she didn't find a solution.

Then she saw the tree, a lone cottonwood waving in the soft breeze as if beckoning to her. Jenn eyed the sturdy tree for a moment, an idea forming in her head. A *bad* idea, probably, but what other choices did she have?

Sliding the reins back over Silver's head, Jenn led him to the base of the tree and tied the reins to one of the lower branches.

Trees she could climb. Horses not so much. But if she could climb onto a branch high enough to be over the horse, but not so far as to make some sort of crazy leap…

She didn't give herself time to think up all the disadvantages of her plan. She scampered up onto the middle branches with the same ease she'd done in childhood.

But that was the easy part. Still holding tight to the tree trunk, she used one foot to test the strength of the branch nearest the horse. It gave a little, but held.

"Okay, then," she muttered to herself. "Time to see if I still remember how to play on the monkey bars."

She eyed the horse one more time, attempting to

judge the distance from the branch to the saddle. Then, holding her breath, she swung out onto the branch, dangling directly over the horse.

Her plan had worked! Or at least she thought it had, before she heard the dry, crackling snap of the branch above her breaking. She had no more time to steady herself or position herself over the saddle before she came tumbling down—right onto the saddle.

"Whoa," she said aloud, both to steady the dancing horse and as an exclamation of the pain she felt. But she was in the saddle, and a sense of elation rushed over her, making her already adrenaline-soaked nerves stand on end.

She nudged the horse forward with her knees, until she could reach the reins still tied to a lower branch of the tree. It didn't take much to loosen them, though getting them back over the horse's neck was a bit problematic.

It was only a moment before she'd turned the horse toward the ranch, giving one backward glance at the ravine where Johnny still lay, in God only knew what condition.

Literally, God only knew.

Chapter Ten

Johnny groaned. He didn't know how much time had passed, or how many times he'd drifted in and out of consciousness. Once Jenn was gone, he'd tried to sit up, but the pain that cut through the back of his head was like a sharp blade, so he lay back down again to wait.

It was hot, and he was thirsty. He knew enough to take only small sips of water at a time, but since he was lying down, he had to pour the water into his mouth from the canteen, and he was certain he dropped more water down his shirtfront than into his mouth.

But what was really worrying him most wasn't his condition, or his safety.

It was Jenn.

She'd only learned to ride today. How would she fare getting back to the ranch on her own? Silver was a reliable horse, but he was also a big one. Johnny wasn't even sure she could mount him on her own.

Presumably she knew her way back to the ranch, having been here so often, but he didn't know for sure.

The mere idea of Jenn getting lost was more terrifying to him than the thought of no one coming to his aid.

What if Jenn *did* get lost and no one came to *her* aid?

It would be a couple of hours before anyone would miss them, and by then dusk would be approaching. It would be hard for the family to look for them in the dark, though Johnny knew they'd try.

He had to get up, to get back to his horse and find Jenn. He sat up, and then winced at the blinding pain stabbing through his head. The earth spun around him. Lights turned to shades of gray as blackness engulfed him.

He wasn't going anywhere.

Jenn managed a slow canter, surprised at how easy it was to remain balanced on Silver once she'd gotten used to the easy, somehow comforting rocking motion. It wouldn't take her much time at all to reach the ranch house at this speed.

Johnny would be safe.

Johnny.

What had he meant by his statement—that he prayed with his eyes open? She half thought he was delirious, but deep in her gut she knew his words had been coherent. And serious.

He was trying to tell her something.

And then it hit her.

He prayed with his *eyes open*. Literally.

Which meant he'd observed that she wasn't praying at all. She'd once asked him if he was a Christian, way back on the first day they'd met, but Johnny had never pursued the same subject with her, a point for which she'd been thankful.

So why did Johnny pick now of all times to bring it up? She'd only been saying something random in order to comfort him, not to start a theological debate on the merits of Christian belief.

She thought it didn't matter, but she'd been wrong about so much, why should this be any different?

Johnny obviously *did* care about her relationship— or lack of one—with God. It mattered to him enough to confront her when he might even be dying.

The thought of Johnny dying was almost more than she could bear. Of course, Christians believed they were going to a better place, not simply having their life snuffed out like a candle.

But Jenn didn't want Johnny in heaven. She wanted him with *her*.

"It's not fair," she said aloud, realizing only after the words were spoken that she was yelling into the wind. "You let this happen, God. You let *all* this happen. Maybe I deserved what Duke did to me. I wasn't being faithful to You, and we both know it.

"But Johnny? He's a good man—honest and decent and...and a Christian!" she stammered. "And now Johnny's hurt, maybe dying. What kind of God are You?"

Tears streamed down her cheeks but were brushed away by the wind. Fury had risen to such intensity in her, she thought she might spontaneously combust. Never had she felt such agony ripping up her insides, not even with Duke.

And then it struck her, as hard and as deep as a bolt of lightening.

She was talking to God.

The God she didn't believe existed.

Or did she?

She was certainly furious with Him now, so angry she wanted to lash out at something.

Someone.

She urged the horse forward into a gallop, appalled at what she'd discovered about herself. She believed in God, all right. And she blamed Him for everything.

It was all God's fault. All of it. Every bad thing that had happened to her. To those in her family. To the kids she worked with.

To Johnny.

And yet, so many of those nearest and dearest to her were believers and loved the Lord with all their heart, strength and mind. She couldn't reconcile it. How could that be?

Her tears had abated, along with her fury, her anger spent and her voice hoarse from yelling. She slowed Silver to a trot, knowing the ranch house was over the next knoll and she could soon send help for Johnny.

She didn't know much scripture, but part of a verse kept repeating itself in her head, despite her constant denial.

I am with you always.

What about when Duke had backhanded her through the bay window?

I am with you always.

What about Johnny, lying in a ditch, terribly hurt or maybe even dying?

And suddenly she knew. She knew it with the same certainty as if she'd been slapped in the face or punched in the gut, yet the realization in her heart had come softly. Silently.

She'd been taught all the right principles and, perhaps

more importantly, had seen those principles lived out in faith by her family's love in action. Yes, it was true she had been a victim of Duke's cruelty, but instead of turning to God for solace, she'd run away.

From her family. Her home. Her God.

Her God.

She wasn't sure what that meant, but the peace that swept over her at that moment was as indefinable as it was sure and certain.

She had no more time to ponder her thoughts or relish the peace in her soul, for she had reached the ranch house and pulled up in front of it. Most of her family was already outside and running toward her. They must have sensed something was wrong.

She slid off Silver, tossing the reins to her brother. "Dad, Mom, get the four-wheeler. Johnny's been hurt."

Scotty had fetched the country doctor from the nearest town. The doctor carefully examined Johnny's head and taped up a couple bruised ribs. A mild concussion was the worst of it, the doctor pronounced. Nothing to worry about. A couple days in bed and he'd be right as rain.

It was when the doctor shook Jenn's hand that she realized her arms were exposed and her family was all around. There was no hiding the truth now.

She wanted to run away from the situation, curl up in a blanket and never come out, but she knew it was too late. By the looks on their faces, a sympathetic mixture of shock and compassion, it was all too obvious what they were thinking.

There was nowhere to hide.

At first, no one said a thing. Scotty excused himself

with a tip of his hat, explaining that he needed to rub
the horses down.

With a sigh, Jenn sat down on the couch. Her mother
and father seated themselves on each side of her, Mom's
arm around her waist and Dad's around her shoulders.
Granny and Auntie Myra pulled chairs in close, each of
them also reaching out to touch her in some way—
Auntie Myra with a shaky palm on Jenn's knee, and
Granny gently but firmly taking one of her hands.
Granddad remained standing, pacing back and forth, his
hands clasped behind his back and his face grim.

With courage she didn't think she possessed, Jenn
looked every one of them straight in the eye, one by one.
She felt like a suspect in a police investigation, with all
eyes on her, as if waiting for a confession.

She wasn't a criminal. She was a victim. Yet that was
exactly what she needed to do.

Confess.

Tell the truth for once.

She held her arms up so everyone could see the
ragged scars clearly in the muted light of the late afternoon sunshine, barely glowing through the living room
windows. Slowly, she turned her arms over so her family, so dear to her now more than ever, could see the full
extent of the damage.

Would they hate her when they knew the full story?

Jenn knew better. Her family was the most forgiving
of any people she'd ever known. But that deep, persist-
ent fear that belonged to the latent child who'd been
afraid to go home, was resurfacing with a vengeance.

Swallowing with difficulty, she struggled to form an
explanation. "These are from—well…" She paused and

gasped for breath. "The truth is, a long time ago, I was pushed from a bay window."

Granny's eyes narrowed. "By whom?" she asked, sounding for all the world like she was going to take a sawed-off shotgun and blast the culprit's head off.

Her mother's grasp tightened around her waist, and for a moment Jenn wished she'd used the word *fallen* instead of *pushed.* But she was done lying, even though she knew the truth would bring more hurt to her beloved family members than in her worst nightmares.

In a way, this *was* her worst nightmare.

"Who did this?" Granny asked again.

Granddad hovered over Granny's shoulder now, his face looking equally sober and angry. It was as much of an emotional expression as she'd ever seen on the old man's face, and Jenn cringed that she'd been the one to put it there.

But then again, she had it coming to her, didn't she? Granddad—the whole family—had every right to be angry with her.

"It was a long time ago," Jenn repeated, her voice cracking. Her heart pumped rapidly, echoing into her head.

"That is why you left home so suddenly," her mother said softly. Jenn could hear the agony of the statement, and it pierced her heart. At the time, she hadn't even considered what pain and anguish she might be causing her family by her sudden flight to Denver. Her only thoughts had been for herself.

"It is," Jenn acknowledged with a slight nod.

"But you were just a teenager," Auntie Myra said, tears running down her face. "Oh, you poor, poor girl. Why didn't you come to us, sweetheart?"

"It doesn't even look like you went to a doctor for those," Granddad said, and for once, his voice didn't carry its usual gruffness.

Jenn looked up at him in surprise. Granddad's eyes were so full of compassion and understanding, Jenn felt even worse than she did before.

Her family loved her unconditionally. She could see that now. If only she'd been able to see that when she was a stupid, naive teenager.

"I'm sure it's no secret to you all that I ran with a bad crowd when I was a teenager. What you didn't know of was my relationship with a certain man," Jenn continued her explanation, revealing every awful detail to her family.

"Why didn't you come to us?" Mom asked, her voice low and rough with emotion when Jenn finished her story.

"I was too ashamed to face any of you. And I knew you'd tell me to rely on my faith. Only, I didn't have any faith. I couldn't find it in my heart to believe there was a God who would just sit back and let such horrible things happen in the world."

She dropped her gaze to her lap, waiting for the judgment she deserved. She'd made one bad mistake after another, and she'd just confessed to her own lack of faith in God. That had to be the worst of it for her family.

No one spoke for the longest time. Jenn squeezed her eyes closed against the tears burning there.

"Jenn," Granny said softly, taking her other hand and squeezing both. "Jenn, look at me."

Jenn raised her head. Granny's eyes were full of compassion and kindness.

No condemnation, no censure.

Only love.

Jenn looked around. Everyone met her gaze square-on, and there wasn't a hint of judgment in any of their eyes.

"You must think I'm a real hypocrite," she said, her voice full of self-loathing.

"We think," stated Granddad clearly, "that you have been through enough."

"We love you, Jenn," her father said. "All of us do. When you go back to Denver, go back with that knowledge in your heart."

Jenn smiled softly through her tears. She hadn't given her family enough credit. Not when she was a teenager, and not now. "There is one more thing I'll be taking back to Denver with me."

"Johnny?" asked Auntie Myra, some of the old glow returning to her eyes, though the tears had not yet dried on her rosy cheeks.

Jenn shook her head emphatically. "God."

Chapter Eleven

Johnny was a bit uncomfortable with Jenn's family hovering over him as if he were facing a terminal illness and not just a bruised ego. He did, though, enjoy Jenn's company. She rarely left his side, and then usually only to get him something to eat or an extra pillow to make him more comfortable.

He slept way past sunup, and when he awoke, he found Jenn dozing in a chair next to his bed, an open bible in her lap.

A bible.

Thank You, Lord, for the good that has come from this accident. Thank You for reaching Jenn with Your love and compassion. Her soul is so desperately in need, and only You can fill the void. Help her to see Your truth and feel Your love.

"Jesus can help you, Jenn," he whispered through a dry throat and cracked lips.

Jenn jumped, her bible falling to the floor at her feet as she used the palm of her hand to wipe the sleep from her beautiful blue eyes. Johnny remembered the first time he'd seen her, all made up and fancy. She looked as good to him now—better, even—with a fresh face and sleep-tousled hair.

Or lack of sleep. Johnny doubted she'd had much rest that night, as uncomfortable as that pinewood desk chair was.

"I really think you should go into Cheyenne and get a CAT scan done," Jenn said, as Johnny yawned widely. He wondered if she was deliberately changing the subject.

Maybe she was. But he'd let it drop for now, knowing he'd bring it up again when he was feeling better.

"No need." His voice sounded gravelly even to his own ears. He cleared his throat.

With a soft smile, she leaned over and smoothed the hair back over his brow. He closed his eyes again, savoring the sensation of her soft fingertips against his skin, and the sweet, soft floral scent that always accompanied Jenn's presence.

"If it's a money issue, I'll take care of it. It's my fault you hurt yourself in the first place," she said gently.

Johnny lurched up in bed, spilling the mug of coffee on the nightstand. The jolt of pain in his head was nothing compared to the shock he'd just experienced in his heart.

"*Your* fault? How do you figure?"

She refused to meet his gaze. "You were trying to save my neck when you fell. I would have gone right off that ravine, otherwise."

Johnny quirked a grin. "And I suppose you were galloping toward that ravine for the fun of it?"

"Of course not. A rattlesnake spooked Silver and off

he went. I had absolutely no control over the beast. It was all I could do to hang on."

Johnny nodded briskly, and then winced as pain shot through his temple. "So how do you figure it's your fault, darlin'?"

"You and your chivalrous streak," she said with a shake of her head that made her hair bounce delightfully. "First you gallantly agree to play the role of my significant other for the sake of my ego, and then you race your horse in front of mine to keep me from plunging to my death."

"First off, Jenn," Johnny said patiently, reaching for her hand, "I had as much to benefit from our—uh, mutual friendship as you. And second, I think you're being overdramatic."

She glared at him. "Am I?"

Johnny shrugged, but the movement hurt his ribs and he winced from the pain. "Silver probably would've turned anyway. Horses don't have death wishes any more than humans do."

"So there was no reason for you to ride in front of me, is that what you're saying?" she asked caustically, casting out his logic.

"Just call it an extra precaution," he said with a grin.

"Which left you at the bottom of a ravine with a hard knock to the head."

"Maybe God thought I needed to have a good conk on the head," he joked, then sobered when Jenn's expression became serious.

"About that, Johnny. I—"

He stopped her from completing her sentence. "You don't owe me an explanation."

"No," she agreed. "But I'm going to give you one anyway." She picked up the bible from where it had fallen and carefully placed it on the desk. "You were right about my faith. Rather, my lack of faith."

"When did I say that?"

"You didn't. Not exactly, anyway. But I was aware you knew I was faking it for my family's sake. I think they knew, as well, but were waiting for me to have the courage to face up to it."

"And now?"

"Well, let's just say it was a long ride back to the ranch. I *am* a coward. I was afraid to face myself. Even worse, I was afraid to face God."

Despite the ache in his head, Johnny pushed himself up until he was sitting at the edge of the bed, glad he was still clothed in the jeans he'd been wearing the day before, though now he wore only a loose T-shirt over his bandaged ribs.

"Come here," he said tenderly, reaching his arms to her.

Jenn hesitated only a moment, before shifting to a spot beside him where she could rest her head on his broad shoulder and hear the comforting beat of his heart.

It hurt a little to have Jenn leaning against his ribs, but Johnny didn't care. He wanted her in his arms.

They stayed that way, silently, for a few moments until Jenn shifted so she could look into Johnny's eyes. He grimaced when she bumped his ribs. "I'm sorry," she said quickly, shifting away from him so she wouldn't accidentally bump him again.

"Woman, will you stop apologizing for every little thing?" Johnny asked through gritted teeth. His gaze was full of amusement, and he chuckled.

Jenn laughed with him. "I'm embarrassed to say I yelled in anger at the Almighty God."

"He understands," Johnny said, stroking her hair off her face.

She looked away. "I know that now."

Johnny reached for her hands and kissed her knuckles. "I'm so happy, I think I might just jump up and dance."

"I don't suggest that in your current condition," Jenn said with a laugh.

Suddenly Johnny's eyes became serious as he looked down at her hands, which he still held gently in his.

"What is it?" she asked, her heart nearly stopping at the seriousness in his expression.

"Your arms. They aren't covered." He brushed his fingertips along the scars of one of Jenn's arms.

She pulled away. She didn't want Johnny looking at her like that, full of pity and concern.

"My long-sleeved shirt was your pillow in the ravine," she stated bluntly. "My secret is out."

"One of them, at least," he reminded her soberly. "How did your family take it?"

"Like I should have expected them to. As they would have years ago, when the accident first happened, if I'd just had the nerve to come forward."

"With love, care and concern," Johnny said softly. "You've got a real special family, Jenn."

Tears blurred her vision, but she didn't brush them away. "I do. This time with you has shown me how much they mean to me."

"And how much you mean to them."

"That, too." Jenn nodded. "Which brings up another point."

Johnny said nothing, though his gaze was questioning hers.

"My family needs to know the truth, Johnny. The whole truth. About us, I mean. I'm ready to come clean about it. Don't worry—I'll let them know the entire blame falls on my shoulders."

"Oh, no, it doesn't," he said determinedly.

"It does," she argued. "It was my dumb idea in the first place, sending myself flowers. I don't know what I was thinking. It's not like I could have kept up the ruse for two whole weeks, with or without a real man at my side. But then you showed up. My Johnny."

"You would have confessed the truth at the beginning if it weren't for me," Johnny reminded her, reaching once again for her hand. This time she didn't pull away, and Johnny stroked her palm with the pad of his thumb. Her skin was so soft and smooth, Johnny never wanted to let her go.

Ever.

"If I hadn't put my arm around you when I did," he continued, "you would have told the truth right then. It was my own foolishness that got us into this mess. I was so eager to see how a real family functioned that I compromised my integrity. And yours. I'm deeply sorry for that, more than you know."

Jenn's blue eyes were glistening with tears. "I've never met a man like you."

"I've been waiting my whole life to meet a woman like you," he countered, then realized belatedly what he had said.

Every word of it was true, but he sure shouldn't have spoken his thoughts aloud.

He was even more certain of his thoughtless blunder when Jenn's face went suddenly pale. She looked like she might fall over. Johnny steadied her by the elbow.

"What did you say?" she whispered, her voice ragged with emotion.

Johnny pinched his lips together, wishing he'd managed that particular action a moment sooner. But Jenn deserved to hear the truth, and since he'd already made his spontaneous declaration, he had to say something to back it up, to let Jenn know once and for all how he really felt about her.

No more lies.

"Do you remember the day of the picnic?" he asked in a voice so gentle he would have used it on an unbroken filly.

She nodded.

"I told you I would never hurt you."

"I remember."

She wouldn't meet his gaze, so he reached out his hand, brushing two fingers down her cheek before tipping her chin up so she would have no choice but to look at him and see the truth in his eyes.

"I meant it then, and I mean it now."

Jenn stood suddenly and walked away from him, jamming her hands into the pockets of her blue jeans as she stared unseeingly out the east window. "I know you do."

What this man could do to her with a look was almost more than Jenn could bear. And when he put words to those unspoken expressions, it became too much for her.

She didn't know what to think, how to feel. Johnny

had stirred emotions she didn't even know existed. He'd won her trust. Despite her past, she believed him when he said he'd never hurt her.

That was probably the worst part of it, she thought miserably. He *was* going to hurt her—when he walked out the door of her family's ranch house for the last time and she would never see him again.

"Jenn. Look at me," he softly urged.

She was afraid to turn, to see the sincerity in his gaze, but found herself helpless to do otherwise.

"Stop me if this is too much for you," he said, wincing as he stood.

"Sit down, Johnny. You're going to hurt yourself." She was glad to have something to say that didn't have to do with what she was feeling right now.

He groaned but did as she asked. "All right. If you promise to hear me out."

She wrapped her arms around herself as if for protection, but nodded briskly before she could think better of it. She owed him that courtesy.

"I had good motives for sticking around here and masking as your boyfriend," he said, then shook his head. "But it was not well played. I never should have forced your hand."

"You said that already," she reminded him.

"I did, didn't I?" He chuckled, and then grasped at his rib cage. "My point is, somewhere all this became… more than that for me."

He paused and jammed his fingers through his tousled locks. "I truly care for you, Jenn. I admire so much about you, and I want to know more. The bottom line is that I don't want this to end when the reunion is over."

Neither do I, Jenn thought, turning back to the window so Johnny couldn't read her expression.

"Now, I know you've been through a lot, and I don't want to chase you off with my words, but I have to speak what I feel. I want to see you again after this week is over. Do you think that's possible?"

If there was one thing Jenn had learned in her time with Johnny, it was that anything was possible.

And this request was something she wanted, too. *Needed.* To move on with her life, maybe have the first real relationship she'd ever had with a man, even if it had started out as a lie.

Who knew what the future held for them?

She couldn't answer with words, but she turned to face him, allowing him to see the tears now coursing down her cheeks as she smiled and nodded.

His answering smile lit up the whole room, assuring her beyond words she was doing the right thing to trust this man.

Jenn was enjoying a steaming cup of coffee in the window nook when the doorbell rang. Granny, Auntie Myra and Jenn's mother, she knew, were all quilting on the back porch, so she set her mug on the nearest end table and went to answer the door.

She couldn't have been more surprised by the man on the other side of the door if he had been purple and sporting a pair of antennae.

The first thing she noticed was his suit, a silk tie, and even a well-placed silk handkerchief in his jacket pocket.

In Wyoming.

Slowly, her gaze rose to the man's face. Close-cropped blond hair, blue eyes, clean-shaven, a nice smile. And an expression that bore witness to his feeling out of place. Jenn almost wanted to laugh, if the man standing in her doorway didn't look so serious.

He shifted from one foot to the other, rubbing his hands in front of him. "Good afternoon," he said, his voice a pleasant tenor.

"Hi," Jenn replied, raising her eyebrows and smiling at him. "Can I help you?"

"I'm sorry to bother you," the man began hesitantly, "but I am looking for a colleague of mine. A Mr. Jonathan Whitcomb."

"I'm sorry for your trouble, but there's no one by that name here." She started to close the door when the man barred it with his hand. Surprised, Jenn opened the door back up, gazing expectantly at the well-dressed man.

"I understand," the man started, then paused. "That is, I think he may be going under the alias Johnny Barnes."

Jenn's heart stopped cold.

Her Johnny Barnes? What could this man possibly want with him?

"I think you'd better come inside," Jenn said, opening the door wider and ushering the blond man into the ranch house.

"Thank you," he said. "My name is Blake Edwards III, but most people just call me Trey."

"Glad to meet you, Trey. I'm Jenn Washington. Now why don't you sit down and tell me exactly why you're looking for Johnny Barnes."

Trey ruffled his fingers through his hair, but somehow managed not to displace a single strand. He looked every inch the high-classed businessman, as different as night and day from her sweet, unassuming Johnny.

Jenn seated herself on the sofa and gestured to the chocolate-colored armchair across from her. It occurred to her that this was where she'd had her first conversation with Johnny, when she thought him nothing more than an ignorant cowboy.

How much had changed in such a short time.

"Perhaps I should start at the beginning," he said, seating himself and leaning forward on his elbows, clasping his hands in front of him. "My business partner and I own the Zandor Corporation. Specifically, the Zandor computer software system. Perhaps you've heard of it?"

Of course Jenn had. It was only the top of the line business software company in the world.

Come to think of it, she'd heard of Jonathan Whitcomb, as well. She'd read about him in the papers. Teenage prodigy of some sort, she remembered. He'd started his company at the age of sixteen and it had exploded on the market.

"What does this have to do with Johnny?" she asked again.

"He's here, then," Trey said, sounding relieved. "It's taken me a great deal of time and expense to track him down."

"I'm afraid you'll be disappointed, then," Jenn said. "I don't mean to discourage you, but I'm afraid there's been a mistake. The man I know as Johnny Barnes couldn't possibly be your business partner, Jonathan Whitcomb."

Trey frowned. "And why is that?"

Jenn chuckled. "Trust me. The man I'm talking about

wouldn't be caught dead in a business suit. He's been wrangling on the Wyoming range all summer."

"So that's where he went." The glimmer of hope returned to Trey's eyes. "He just up and left, saying he had to get away from it all for a while. Didn't tell me where he was going or anything. I've been going crazy, trying to run the company without him."

"I still don't think—" Jenn began, but was interrupted from the door to the kitchen.

"I thought I heard the doorbell ring." It was Johnny, looking a bit peaked and clutching at his rib cage, but up on his feet. "What, did you get another delivery of flowers while I…"

His sentence drifted off to nothing as his eyes made contact with Trey's. If Johnny had looked a bit weak in the knees before, he now looked as if he'd fall down flat on his face.

Without thinking, Jenn moved to his side, slipping her arm around his waist to support him. She was about to tell him he shouldn't be out of bed when his next word stopped her cold.

"Trey."

"Jonathan."

"What are you doing here?" Johnny's voice was as hard and cold as she'd ever heard it. He stiffened noticeably in her arms.

Jonathan?

Jenn couldn't wrap her mind around it. Her cowboy, the man she'd given her trust to, a man she might even be starting to fall in love with, wasn't really a cowboy at all?

No way.

It couldn't be.

Her arms still around his waist, she stared up at Johnny, but though he rested his arm around her shoulders, he refused to look her in the eye, choosing rather to glare at the newcomer.

So it was true, then. Johnny's actions were speaking far louder than any words he could have said, and guilt, not denial, was written plainly on his face.

Johnny Barnes, wrangler, was actually Jonathan Whitcomb, millionaire computer prodigy.

Which meant he'd been lying to her from the moment they'd met.

Now she was the one to stiffen. How could he have done this to her?

Her mind raced through all the special moments she and Johnny had shared—the picnic, the horse ride. She'd shared her deepest, most intimate secrets with him.

She'd trusted him.

Anger and betrayal rushed hotly through her veins, an angry haze shadowing her sight. She opened her mouth, trying to breathe, trying to speak, but then clamped her jaw closed again. She had a million and one things she wanted to say to Johnny—Jonathan—right now. She wanted to push him away, scream at him, do something to show the agony she was feeling at her heart being shattered into a million pieces.

She'd *trusted* him.

What a fool she'd been.

There was so much she wanted to say, but she ground her teeth with the effort to remain silent, unwilling to lose what little poise she still possessed.

She would not voice those thoughts. Not now, anyway, with company in the house. She had that much dignity left.

She unwrapped herself from Johnny and turned toward him, knowing he could hear the anger in her voice, even if he refused to look at her face. "I'll leave you to your friend, *Jonathan*," she whispered harshly. "I'm sure you two have a lot of catching up to do."

She twirled around on her toes and, breathing deeply, tried to make a slow, steady exit from the room, her chin held high. She would not dignify the moment by giving him a chance to respond—but she would not run away from him, either.

It was only when she reached the safety of her room and had closed the door behind her that she broke down, sliding to the floor in a crumpled heap, with the cold, wooden door for support, crying for a man she now realized she never really knew at all.

Chapter Twelve

Johnny strode to the couch and sat down opposite his friend. "What are you doing here?" he asked through gritted teeth. "You may just have ruined everything."

Trey chuckled. "What everything?"

"My life," answered Johnny, deadly serious.

"Don't you think that's being a little overdramatic?" Trey asked. "After all, you were the one who left me high and dry without a word. I had no idea where to find you, even in an emergency."

"Was there?"

"Was there what?"

"An emergency."

The blond-haired man frowned, his cheeks staining with color. "Well, no. But I don't see how you could just walk out of your job like that. We've been best friends since childhood. Doesn't that mean anything to you?"

"Of course it does," Johnny said with a shake of his head. "But I couldn't handle it anymore. I've—*we've*—been working nonstop since we were sixteen. We missed being kids. Doesn't that ever bother you?"

Trey's eyebrows shot up. "Yeah, but look at the money we've made."

Johnny slammed his palms down on his knees in frustration. "I don't care about the money. I was going crazy in New York. I needed a break, and I knew if I told you what I was going to do, you'd either talk me out of it or tail me until I relented. And I wasn't so far off, now was I?"

Trey just stared at him, stunned.

Johnny jammed his fingers into his hair. Whatever mess he was in now was his own making. It wasn't Trey's fault Johnny had dropped off the planet without leaving word of his whereabouts. It had seemed a good idea at the time—but then again, so did a lot of the actions he'd made recently, actions he now regretted with all his heart.

Especially where Jenn was concerned.

But first he owed Trey an apology. His friend was looking at him as if he'd grown a third nose, and rightly so. They had been close, as Trey had pointed out, since they were kids, and they'd built their company from the ground up.

"I'm sorry," Johnny said contritely. "I'm taking my frustration out on you and that's not right."

"I can see you're upset, buddy. I'm sorry if I've made things difficult for you. I've obviously come at a bad time, if that pretty woman who just stalked from the room is any indication. Maybe I should just leave."

"Not until I explain things to you," Johnny said, punching his fist into his palm. "I owe you that much, at least. I'm in a world of trouble, especially with Jenn, but it's all my own doing."

"So, then, what's up?" Trey said, leaning back in the

armchair. "I don't understand any of this. Why did you disappear the way you did?"

"Like I said, I short-circuited. Don't you ever feel like we missed out on something, starting our company as early as we did?"

Trey shrugged. "Yeah, I guess we did. I mean, rooming with you in college was fun and all, but we didn't do much, other than work and study, did we?"

"That's an understatement. So you understand why I needed a break, then?"

Trey shook his head. "Not entirely. We're living our dreams, Jonathan, doing all the things we talked about as kids. We travel the world, attend fancy parties, and run a multibillion-dollar corporation."

Johnny shook his head vehemently. "I hate those parties. And while I admit I enjoy traveling, it's not exactly like a vacation when you're on business, is it?"

"Guess not," Trey conceded.

"I'm finding that, lately, the things I thought were important don't hold the same sparkle they used to. My priorities," Johnny said softly, gazing at his hands, "have changed."

Trey glanced at the French doors where Jenn had exited. "You have a new girlfriend?"

Johnny scowled in earnest. "Can we just leave her out of this?"

Trey shrugged. "I guess."

"I didn't leave because of her. I didn't even know her at the time," Johnny said, with a weary sigh. He wrapped an arm around his rib cage, which was aching mercilessly. Or maybe the ache was deeper inside.

He tried not to think about it. Not now. "I hired on

for the summer as a wrangler at a Wyoming ranch. I thought it'd be good for me to sleep out under the stars for a change."

Trey made a face. "Ugh. Not my idea of a good time, but whatever. I've got to say, buddy, you aren't looking so good right now. Are you feeling all right?"

Johnny nodded, knowing he was unable to hide the misery of his expression. "I'm okay."

Trey apparently chose to take Johnny's word at face value. "Glad to hear it. Now, what I want to know is, when are you coming back to New York?"

Johnny glanced at the door where Jenn had left moments earlier and winced inwardly. If he had any sense in him at all, he'd run back to New York this instant, with his tail tucked between his legs. He'd made a huge mess of things all around. It would be the easiest thing in the world to just up and leave—maybe even easiest for Jenn, too, in the long run. She couldn't be very happy with him right now, that was for sure.

Then again, he'd never been a man to run away from his problems, especially those he'd brought upon himself. He would stay this one out, though he had little hope of regaining what trust he'd built with Jenn.

Johnny scrubbed a hand down his face, vaguely realizing he was unshaven. Between that and the way he still favored his rib cage, it was no wonder Trey thought he wasn't at the top of his game.

Johnny caught and held Trey's gaze. "I can't leave right now. I have some unfinished business to take care of here."

"Meaning the woman."

"Meaning a lot of things," Johnny snapped back, angry that his friend should bear such a cavalier attitude toward Jenn. "Up to and including the fact that I have another month left of wrangling. I signed a contract."

"Which our lawyers can easily handle."

"I gave my word, Trey. Right now, that doesn't count for very much. I'm not going to make it any worse than it already is by breaking my contract with the Double Y."

"So you're not coming back."

"I didn't say that. Just not yet."

"I just don't like being left with all the responsibility."

"Tell you what," Johnny offered. "When I get back to New York in a month, I'll let *you* take some time off for a change."

"I don't need—" Trey began, but Johnny cut him off, raising his palms to halt Trey's words.

"Nonnegotiable," Johnny insisted. "You've worked every bit as hard as I have. You deserve a vacation and you're going to get one."

Trey shrugged. "I don't get you, Jonathan. I finally find you, and here you are, way out in the middle of Wyoming, looking like a cowboy, working like one. What's up with that?"

"I obviously can't explain it, at least to you. It was just something I had to do. Can we leave it at that?"

"Yes, if that's what you want."

"It's what I need. We can talk about it more later, when I get back to work. In the meantime, I appreciate you covering for me. I shouldn't have left without telling you where I was going, and I apologize again for that."

Johnny took a piece of paper from one of the side tables and jotted down a telephone number. "You can reach me here if I'm not out on the range, or leave a message if I am. You can also e-mail me. I've been avoiding work mail, but I promise I'll check my messages often and get back to you as soon as possible."

Trey shook his head skeptically, then stood and offered his hand to Johnny. "I wish you the best, pal, with whatever it is you have going."

"Thanks, Trey," Johnny said, and meant it. "I promise I'll make it up to you."

"I'm sure you will," Trey answered dryly. "In the meantime, tell that pretty blonde it was nice to meet her for me, will you?"

This time Johnny cringed outwardly. That "pretty blonde" was probably never going to speak to him again, and if she did, he doubted he'd get the opportunity to pass along Trey's message to her.

He had the distinct feeling Jenn was never going to listen to a word he had to say about anything.

Ever.

As soon as he saw Trey off, Johnny went straight to Jenn's room, figuring, as likely as not, she'd holed herself up in there. Maybe permanently.

As he expected, Jenn's door was closed. He gently tried the handle just to see if it gave, but not surprisingly, it was locked. He listened quietly, his ear to the door, and thought he heard soft sobbing from the other side.

It tore up his insides to know *he* was the reason Jenn was crying. He took a deep breath and knocked. He couldn't make things right if he didn't face her head-on.

"Jenn, it's Johnny," he said, his voice just over a whisper. "Let me come in. I need to answer all your questions, darlin'."

At first there was no answer. When he knocked again, he heard movement on the other side of the door, but still no answer.

"Just go away," Jenn answered through the closed door the third time he knocked. "I don't want to talk to you. You don't have to answer to me."

"Oh, yes, I do," he replied, resting his forehead and both palms against the cool oak of the door. "Please. Just open up the door, will you? I need to explain what is going on here."

"You don't *need* to do anything, mister," she replied bitterly. "Just leave me alone."

Johnny sighed miserably but turned away from the door. Who could blame Jenn if she didn't want to talk to him? He could hardly stand his *own* presence right now. He couldn't imagine how she felt.

Defeated, he trudged back to his own room, closing the door behind him and dropping painfully to his knees beside the bed.

It was a long, excruciating few minutes before he could pray. Images of Jenn rushed through his mind. The first moment he'd seen her. Her gorgeous blue eyes gleaming with unshed tears as she told him about her past. Her joy when she shared her new love of the Lord with him.

And he'd ruined everything.

He'd meant to tell her the truth a dozen times, yet he had stalled, convincing himself the moment wasn't right, that she wasn't quite ready to hear what he had to say.

He didn't know what really held him up. Jenn worked in the city, loved everything about its fast pace.

She only came to the country for her family, and she

clearly didn't like cowboys at all. No doubt, she would have been thrilled to hear he wasn't a wrangler, but rather a successful businessman.

So, why hadn't he told her the truth while there was still the opportunity to do so?

Because, he finally admitted to himself, he'd liked things the way they were. He liked being a humble cowboy and not a jet-setter. He was, he realized, a simple cowboy at heart, no matter what kind of business he ran in New York.

And more than anything in the world, he wanted to hang on to the sweet simplicity of the relationship he'd developed with Jenn.

Except that it had all been based upon a lie.

He groaned. He didn't want to face himself, much less his Heavenly Father. But he couldn't ask forgiveness from Jenn until he'd asked forgiveness from God.

"Dear Lord," he prayed earnestly. *"I've made a royal mess of things. I've deeply hurt a woman I've come to love, and I don't know how to make it right. Be with her, Father, and care for her wounded spirit. I only pray she'll find strength in her new faith in You. I pray that what I've done won't shake her tenuous newfound faith. I know she trusts You now, Lord, and You will never betray her. Let her rest in that confidence now, more than ever. Amen."*

Jenn barricaded herself in her room all day, not even coming out for dinner. She didn't expect Johnny to be at the dinner table, but she didn't want to take that chance. Not until she was ready to face him.

At the moment, she wasn't ready for much of anything. Her thoughts were muddled, her emotions clustered so tight in her chest she thought she might burst from the pain.

Maybe she should just go talk to Johnny, lay it out on the line.

Make him go away.

Yet, the thought of the ranch house without Johnny in it was almost more than she could bear. He had brightened up her whole world with his smile. What would it be like when he was gone?

She'd have to face that inevitability sooner or later, she realized. Just this afternoon, it had sounded like Johnny wanted to pursue a relationship with her, something beyond the farce they'd created.

Something built on truth, not lies.

But Johnny had lied. About himself. About everything. Who knew whether anything he'd ever said to her was true.

There was one way to find out.

Bolstering her confidence, she quietly slipped through the hallway and across the vacant living room to the opposite hallway, where Johnny's bedroom was. She stopped before the door, her hand raised to knock, but paused momentarily, trying to gather her thoughts.

This might be her one and only opportunity to speak her mind. She had the feeling Johnny might be leaving a little earlier than planned. She would have already packed and shipped off if she were him.

She bit her bottom lip until it hurt, concentrating on the physical pain instead of the emotional throbbing of her heart. With a deep breath, she rapped sharply on the door.

She heard Johnny stirring a moment before he said softly, "Come in, Jenn."

He was certainly sure of himself, believing it was her on the other side of the door. That made her anger surge. How dare he presume *anything?*

She slipped through the door, closing it behind her and leaning back on its cool strength. She needed all the support she could get.

Johnny—Jonathan—whatever his real name was, was seated in the chair, an arm sheltering his rib cage. He wasn't looking straight at her, and Jenn could see a muscle working in his jaw.

"Thank you for coming," he said at last, sounding as if he had invited her to a party or something. He hadn't invited her anywhere. *She* had come to *him.*

"Hmmph," she answered, crossing her arms.

"I want to explain."

"I'll just bet you do," she snapped, wondering whether she'd made the right decision confronting Johnny right now, while she was in such a vulnerable emotional state.

"Jenn, please," he pleaded quietly, his midnight-blue gaze finally meeting hers. Gone was the amused quirk of his mouth, replaced by a thin, straight, grim line. "Just listen."

"No, *you* listen, cowboy," Jenn bit back. She had a few things to get off her chest before he launched into whatever pathetic explanation he cared to share.

"Jenn," he groaned.

"I can't believe you lied to me," she said accusingly. "Johnny Barnes? Jonathan Whitcomb? You didn't even tell me your real name.

"Actually, I did," he admitted gravely.

"Oh, yeah. Right. So now I am supposed to believe

your friend Trey, who traveled out here, clear from New York, in order to find you, I might add, was mistaken when he called you Jonathan Whitcomb?"

Johnny jammed his fingers into his black curls. Unlike with his friend Trey, whose similar movement hadn't disturbed a hair on his head, Johnny's action ruffled his dark, curly locks, reminding Jenn of a little boy.

She'd always appreciated the unpredictable, wind-blown look his hair often had. But she didn't want to think about that now. She didn't want to think about the many things which had so completely attracted her to Johnny. Most of it, except perhaps his outward appearance, was a lie. And even that—the cowboy hat and boots—appeared to be a ruse.

"My full name is Jonathan Barnes-Whitcomb. I just dropped the last part when I was with you."

"And you couldn't tell me the truth because…?" she prodded, and then continued before he could say a word. "Because you didn't trust me enough to tell me the truth, that's why. You told me I could trust you, but where was your trust in me?"

She knew her own hurt and pain was flowing through the high-pitched strum of her voice, but she didn't care.

"Was it all a lie, Johnny? Everything you said, everything you did?"

"Jenn, no. I—"

She cut him off again. "I don't want to hear it."

"But—"

"But nothing. You let me—" She paused and sucked in a pained breath. "I told you things I've never told another living soul. And all the while you were hiding your true identity from me."

"That's true, but—"

Jenn held up her hands for silence. "I said I didn't want to hear it. Not from you. Not now. How can I believe a word that comes out of your mouth? I came clean to my family and told them everything. But you…"

Johnny clenched and unclenched his fist around the arm of the chair but remained silent, no longer attempting to jump to his own defense.

Good, Jenn thought. There was no defense for such abominable actions. He might as well save his breath, for all she was concerned.

"I know God wants me to forgive you," she continued testily, "and…and I will. Someday. I don't feel it in my heart right now. I don't feel anything."

She stared at him pointedly. "I don't feel a thing."

Now she was the one who was lying, and she knew it. Did it count that she desperately wanted her words to be true? Oh, what she wouldn't give *not* to care, *not* to feel anything for this man.

Johnny sucked in a deep breath and winced, probably from the pain in his ribs, Jenn thought. Or perhaps from her verbal jabs. Either way was just fine with her right now.

She wanted to hurt him, make him feel some of the pain she was feeling from his betrayal. She knew it wasn't right, that it wasn't what God wanted her to do, but she couldn't seem to help herself.

"Anyway, it doesn't matter, does it?" she hissed. "You'll be gone tomorrow."

"What makes you think I am going anywhere?" he ground out through clenched teeth, his voice coarse.

"Aren't you?"

"No. Not until the end of the week, at least. Face it, Jenn. You're going to have to deal with me sometime in the next three days."

Jenn leveled him with a stare. "No. I don't. I won't. This is my house, cowboy. You're my guest. If I tell you to go, you go."

"I'm Scotty's guest," he reminded her. "And he drove me and Lucy out here in his truck. I couldn't leave even if I wanted to." He paused thoughtfully. "Which I don't."

Jenn felt as if he were backing her up against that cottonwood tree again, as he had at the picnic. But this time she didn't want to stand her ground with him. She wanted to duck and run.

Except, she wasn't the one who should be running. And she would not back down. "Fine. Just stay out of my way. No more lies, Johnny."

"Don't forget, Jenn," Johnny replied bitterly, "The lies started with you."

Johnny clamped his mouth shut the moment he'd said the words, but the damage had already been done. Jenn's face, once red with fury, now drained of color, and she swayed on her feet.

He stood and strode to her side, wrapping his arms around her to keep her from falling, but she made a small squeal of protest and immediately squirmed out of his grasp, bumping into his bad ribs in the process.

He groaned and backed up, clutching at the spot her elbow had hit, wondering if her action had been intentional or simply panic.

Not that it made any difference. He'd promised himself he would not lash back, no matter what she said to him, and then he'd gone and opened his big mouth again. He deserved whatever was coming to him.

The words had just slipped out. Jenn *had* started it. But that didn't make Johnny any less culpable, as well he knew. "Jenn, I'm sorry. I didn't mean it."

She was backing up toward the door, her doe-eyed gaze never leaving his. "Yes, you did."

"No. I—"

"And you're right. This is all my fault. I did this to myself."

"No, Jenn. We both—"

"Just stay out of my way, Johnny. Please?" This time she was pleading, not demanding. Johnny found it almost impossible to bear. His heart was being ripped to shreds, and he felt each and every tug, every tear, more painfully than the bruises on his ribs.

It was better—easier—when she was accusing him. He couldn't bear to see her take the blame upon herself, to see the self-loathing in her eyes and know that he'd put it there.

She wasn't completely without blame, or his words wouldn't have found their mark. But he shouldn't have said anything to begin with.

Jenn had backed all the way to the door. She reached behind her, grasping for the handle without taking her gaze off him. "I'm sorry I got you into this mess," she said softly, unshed tears glistening in her eyes.

He heard the handle click open before he moved, but when he did, it was fast. Two quick strides and his palm was on the door over her head, slamming it closed behind her. He couldn't allow her to leave this way, taking all the blame on herself.

"No way are you walking out that door without hearing my side of the story," he said, his voice a soft rasp. "I'm not going to try to defend my actions, but you need to know the truth. The *whole* truth."

She tipped her chin up defiantly and her eyes locked with his. For the slightest moment, just before she shielded her gaze from his, he saw a plethora of emotions washing through the brilliant blue depths of her eyes.

Pain. Anger. Betrayal.

And what else? Fear?

Johnny stepped back, clenching his fists until his arms were shaking from the effort. What was he doing? He was scaring her with his oafish actions. That was the last thing he wanted to do, now or ever.

What he wanted was to make things right with her, to make her understand that, no matter what he had said, or more to the point, *hadn't* said, he truly cared for her. He wanted to pursue the tenuous relationship they'd built together, not remind her of Duke and the past that had haunted her for so long.

But that was exactly what he was doing, however unintentionally.

Hurting her.

Again.

He stepped back and jammed his fingers through his hair with one hand while gesturing her out the door with the other. "Go," he whispered hoarsely.

Jenn reached for the knob, but her gaze never left his. "I—I'm sorry, Johnny," she stammered weakly, then turned and slipped quietly out the door.

Chapter Thirteen

Jenn was sorrier than she could ever say. She'd marched into Johnny's room and struck him with her words more harshly than a physical blow might have been. Regret mixed with remorse in the pit of her stomach.

Johnny had been wrong for not telling her the truth, or at least the whole truth. But, as he'd so aptly pointed out, she was equally at fault.

More so, even.

She'd started all this. Johnny's reasons for masquerading as a cowboy couldn't be any more complicated than the charade she'd played out with her family. She'd thought she had good reasons, just as Johnny must have, and look where that had gotten her.

No more lies!

God's spirit settled within her the moment her mind was made up. If the snarled web of her life had been woven with deceit, could it possibly be untangled by telling the truth?

Jenn didn't know, but she was about to find out.

She strode into the living room, determined to find

her family and tell them everything. Scotty was the only one present, his legs dangling across the arm of the plush chocolate-colored easy chair, his cowboy hat on his lap, as he watched cartoons on television.

"Still watching baby stuff, I see," Jenn said teasingly, as she entered.

"Funnier than anything else on," Scotty replied, making a face at her. "Better than your soap operas."

"Probably," Jenn admitted, sitting down on the couch across from her brother.

"Huh?" Scotty queried, obviously surprised that his sister was, for once in her life, agreeing with him.

"I just said you are probably right," Jenn repeated.

"Okay. What's going on? Who kidnapped my sister and replaced her with you?"

Jenn sighed. "It's complicated." She stared at her brother for a moment, realizing how much he'd grown up since she'd seen him last. Time moved so fast. Things changed in a heartbeat. She needed to make more of an effort to see her family.

If they ever wanted to see her again after tonight.

"Do me a favor?" she asked.

"Sure, sis."

"Can you round up Mom and Dad for me? Granny and Granddad, too."

"And Auntie Myra?"

Jenn cringed inwardly, knowing Auntie Myra would be the most outspoken of the bunch, and would no doubt have a good deal to say about what Jenn was about to reveal.

"And Auntie Myra," she conceded, with a reluctant shrug of her shoulders.

"What for?"

"I'll tell you when everyone is here."

Scotty planted his hat on his head, tipped the brim at her, and left the room to find the family. It only took him a minute before everyone was gathered, curiosity lining every face in the room.

"What's up, Jenn?" Granny asked, as soon as everyone was sitting. Count on Granny to be the one to cut straight to the chase.

"I just—I have something I need to say," Jenn said, stopping and starting again. "It's about Johnny."

For once, it seemed nobody in her family had anything to say. Jenn wished the floor would open and swallow her. It figured, the one time they were quiet was the one time she desperately wanted to hear voices.

"What about Johnny?" her mother asked, when Jenn didn't immediately continue.

"Well, for starters," Jenn said at last, "His real name isn't Johnny Barnes. It's Jonathan Barnes-Whitcomb."

"As in Jonathan Whitcomb the computer guru?" her dad asked with a low whistle.

"One and the same," Jenn admitted miserably. "He was apparently taking some time off to wrangle over the summer, which is where he met Scotty."

"Hmm," murmured Granddad, cocking an eyebrow. "Shouldn't Johnny be telling us this?"

Jenn nodded. "You're probably right on that account. But I have some things I need to tell you all, and it would be better, or at least clearer, if you understood up front who Johnny really is."

Again, there was a deafening silence in the room, as everyone waited for Jenn to continue.

"The thing is, I need to ask your forgiveness. I will-

fully mislead you all into thinking Johnny and I have—
had—a relationship. The bouquet of roses I received that
first day, well, they weren't from Johnny."

"What do you mean, sweetheart?" Mom asked gently.

Jenn stammered out the entire story. When she finished she looked from face to face. "I'm sorry. I didn't
think—"

"No. You didn't think," Granny answered, cutting
her off.

"But we're glad you've come clean," Mom added,
reaching for Jenn's hand. "It can't be easy for you to
make this kind of admission in front of us all."

"Can you forgive me? For everything I've done, all
the lies I've told?"

"Jenn, honey, of course we can," Mom said softly.
"We've always known that you had some bad things
happen to you in your past, things you never talked
about, until this year."

Of course they knew. She'd left home the day after
high school, not even waiting for September and the
start of college to get away from home.

From her memories of Duke.

From her shame.

Even after she discovered in her college classes that
what had happened to her wasn't her fault, that there
was no shame in being the victim of abuse. Wasn't that
what she told so many battered women on the street,
who were running from their own pasts?

Yet, she'd never quite forgiven herself. Instead, she'd
chosen to blame God and stuff her painful feelings deep
inside her heart, rather than face them and move forward
with her life.

And look where that got her.

Here.

With a family that loved her unconditionally, who were now rallying around her with support and consideration, even when she admitted lying to them.

"Can I ask you a question?" Dad queried, moving to Jenn's other side and dropping a gentle arm over her shoulder.

"You can ask me anything," Jenn answered sincerely.

"Why now? Why did you decide to set things straight tonight?"

"Because," said Jenn, "I discovered I could no longer run from God. I don't want to. I've been so angry for so long. I just don't want to do that anymore. No more running. No more lies. I need to face my life—my whole life—head-on."

Mom kissed her cheek. "Do you know how proud we all are of you? You're a strong, compassionate, caring woman, Jenn."

Her mother's words cut like a knife. Jenn wasn't any of those things. She wasn't strong. And she sure hadn't been acting caring and compassionate, especially to Johnny. She had a feeling she was going to be eating a lot more crow before the week was through.

"And Johnny?" Granny queried, an amused gleam in her eyes.

"Yes," Auntie Myra seconded. "What about our Johnny?"

Jenn shook her head. "I don't know. I'm really confused right now."

Mom laughed and squeezed her hand. "Confused? Or in love?"

"What?" she squawked, standing suddenly to her feet and turning to meet the gazes of each of her family members. They all looked at her expectantly, as if waiting for another confession.

Were her feelings that obvious? Here she'd thought she'd been keeping everything boxed in, when really, they had known about her all along. Maybe better than she knew herself.

"I thank God for having a family like you," she said, hugging her mother and father, who were nearest to her, and then moving on to Granny and Auntie Myra.

"That," quipped Auntie Myra with a short laugh, "most definitely sounded like an abrupt change of subject."

Jenn laughed with her. "It's true. I'm not making any more confessions tonight. But I really meant what I said about you guys. You're the best."

"We think *you're* the best," said Granny, giving Jenn another tight hug.

"Okay, I'm out of here," Scotty said, giving Jenn a peck on the cheek. "This is getting way too mushy for me."

"Hmmph," Granddad added.

"Okay, okay," Jenn conceded. "You're right." She moved to the door and then turned, throwing her family members a kiss with her palm. Suddenly impish, she knew she just had to have the last word, for once.

"I love you, though," she said mischievously, then turned and ran down the hall to her room.

Johnny had been pacing his room all night. He couldn't sleep. He couldn't eat. He couldn't think straight, not since Jenn had come in and railed on him like that.

He'd already packed his saddlebags.

It was time for him to leave.

He was no longer running from anything. Jenn wanted him gone. She'd made that fact perfectly clear. And it wasn't as if he couldn't afford a taxi, even to as remote a spot as this ranch. Scotty would probably be willing to drive Lucy back.

Before he left, though, Johnny had one more thing he needed to do. Picking up his bible, his index finger marking the passage he'd selected, he strode from his room and down the hallway.

He knocked on Jenn's door, but there was no answer. He tried the knob, and it turned. "Jenn?" he called softly. He didn't want to intrude on her privacy. "Jenn? You here?"

When there was no answer, he peeked in the door. The room was empty.

He breathed a sigh of relief. No need to have another scene like the one yesterday. Johnny didn't want to cause her a moment's more grief. Just this one thing and he'd be out of here.

It only took him a moment to do what needed doing. He set his open bible on her bed, took one deep, poignant breath of the floral scent of the woman who occupied the room, and made his exit.

It was time for him to go home.

Never an early riser, Jenn surprised herself by waking with the dawn. Spontaneously, she'd taken a long walk on the ranch in order to clear her head, along a trail which had, to her own surprise, ended in the stable.

"Hey there, Silver," she said, approaching the gray gelding. She grabbed an apple from her pocket, which she'd brought along for her own breakfast, and fed it to the friendly horse, who nickered playfully as he chomped down the fruit.

Jenn laughed as the horse nudged her shoulder, obviously looking for more goodies. "Sorry, boy. That's all I have."

She wasn't afraid of the horse anymore. Not even a little. Her fear had dissipated like dew in the morning sunshine. She might not ever *like* horses that much, but it was nice to know she no longer feared them.

Thanks to Johnny.

She inhaled deeply, enjoying the pungent scent of fresh hay and horse. She used to associate the smell of horses with all that was bad in her life, but now she found a smile lingering on her lips.

Johnny truly had changed everything.

Silver nickered again. Impatiently.

"You're right, boy," she said, more to herself than to the horse. "What am I doing out here? No sense putting off the inevitable. I need to go find Johnny, don't I?"

Silver shifted and bumped her shoulder with his muzzle again. "Yeah, yeah, I get your drift," Jenn said with a laugh. She patted the gray on the neck. "Next time I'll bring more fruit, I promise."

Giving the horse one last pat on the muzzle, she left the stable, determined to find Johnny. First, though, she wanted to go back to her bedroom and spend some time in bible-reading and prayer.

This time, nothing was going to daunt her, nothing would get in the way of telling Johnny all that was in her heart. She needed all of God's good grace to make sure her mouth didn't once again get the best of her.

She paused before the door to her room, her heartbeat increasing markedly. She was certain she'd closed her door when she'd left earlier this morning, but now it was cracked open. She had the oddest feeling she wasn't alone, and half expected Johnny to be waiting inside her room.

She pushed the door back and peered inside.

Empty.

Sighing with relief, she entered her room and closed the door behind her. As much as she wanted to see Johnny, she needed her time with the Lord first.

And then she saw it—a well-worn bible lying open on her pillow. One thing she knew for certain—it wasn't *her* bible. Hers had only recently been opened, and the pages were still neat and crisp. This bible had been used. A lot. Its pages were dog-eared and the leather worn.

Johnny's bible.

She remembered it from the first day he'd come, when he'd so reverently taken his bible from his saddlebag. She remembered the tender way he'd handled the book, running his long, calloused fingers over the cover.

Curiously, she sat on the edge of the bed and picked up the holy book, careful not to lose the page to which it was opened. She inhaled the scent of the soft leather, which reminded her of Johnny.

Johnny the cowboy, anyway.

Glancing down at the bible, she scanned the page. It was opened to the Book of Isaiah. Jenn didn't remember much from the Old Testament, except perhaps a few of the better-known stories she'd learned in Sunday school—Abraham, Isaac, Jacob, Joseph, Moses.

But not Isaiah.

She'd been reading through the gospels, trying to get to know her Savior better through His own words while He was here on earth. She supposed she'd eventually get to the Old Testament. After her change of heart the day Johnny was injured, she was achingly, unquenchably thirsty for God's word, and spent hours every day reading the bible.

Curiosity turned into fervency and she glanced over the open pages. There was something here Johnny wanted her to read. But what was it?

That Johnny had gone to the trouble to leave the passage for her affected her heart in the funniest way, making it flitter around like a swarm of butterflies. She'd thought he might never speak to her again, and with good reason, the way she'd ranted off on him.

Yet, despite their differences, Johnny was still thinking of her, perhaps praying for her. Again, she was struck by his kindness, a trait that had gone so far to restore Jenn's faith in humanity and in men in particular.

And among men, Johnny was the cream of the crop. She knew that now.

Curling up at the head of the bed, a pillow under her elbow, she started reading Isaiah, Chapter 52. It was a beautiful, poetic passage, but Jenn found nothing that jumped off the page at her.

Then she moved on to Isaiah, 53 and suddenly Jenn knew exactly why Johnny had left this particular page open for her. Though written by an Old Testament prophet, the passage was talking, to Jenn's amazement, about Jesus, as surely as the gospels, which had been written after His birth.

A man of sorrows, acquainted with grief. Her Savior

had already trodden the path she walked, and had risen victorious from it. And through Him, she realized with a light heart and joyous spirit, she could do the same.

She kept reading, anxious to learn more.

And then she read words that pierced her more sharply than the double-edged sword her parents had always sworn the word of God to be.

By His stripes we are healed.

His wounds were in many ways similar to the scars Jenn bore on her arms. Jesus, too, had been the victim of a violent, senseless crime.

Well, not senseless, perhaps. Jesus had suffered for her so she wouldn't have to suffer, so she could live her life for Him. That was what Johnny wanted her to see, wanted her to understand.

And she did. She did believe.

She closed the bible and brushed the cover with a reverent hand, then bowed her head to pray. If God could heal her, He could heal the rift she had created between her and Johnny.

All she needed were the right words, and the spirit of God could help her with that. She was sure of it.

Johnny stood on the front porch, his saddlebag, packed and ready, over his left shoulder. With a long sigh, he inhaled the crisp, cool morning air. How he loved the country. He'd miss it when he returned to the stuffy, polluted air of New York.

Not as much as he'd miss being here with the Washingtons, though. And especially not as much as he'd miss Jenn. Time, it was said, healed all wounds, but Johnny wasn't convinced.

It would be a long, long time before he had Jenn Washington out of his system. The way he felt right now, maybe never. She was one special woman—the woman he'd been waiting for all his life.

And because of his lies, he'd never see her again.

Spying the porch swing, he swung his saddlebag to the ground and took a seat. No telling how long it would be before the town car he'd ordered would arrive. This ranch wasn't exactly easy to find. Most of the roads surrounding it weren't even on the map.

Johnny stretched his legs out in front of him and tipped his cowboy hat over his eyes. He didn't think he could rest, but it was worth a try. Every time he closed his eyes he pictured Jenn, laughing, riding a horse, scowling adorably at him with her arms perched on her hips.

He'd memorized her face—every look, every expression. He'd remember her blazing blue eyes as long as he lived.

He wondered if the ache in his heart would ever ease, or whether he was looking at a lifetime of regret.

Regret. He was sure of it.

It only took Jenn a couple of minutes to find Johnny sitting out on the front porch swing, his cowboy hat tipped over his eyes. He was breathing deeply and evenly, and she wondered if he was sleeping.

She tiptoed to his side and stood looking down at him, her heart fluttering wildly. He was so handsome he took her breath away, but that wasn't all that made her heart go wild in her chest.

Not even mostly.

Johnny was the best man Jenn had ever met. He was kind, gentle and loved the Lord with a quiet passion Jenn only hoped she could emulate. He had helped her in so many ways.

She was no longer afraid. Not of horses. Not of God. Not of men.

Most definitely not of Johnny.

She had been kidding herself by thinking she could just walk away from this man. So he had secrets. She wasn't exactly a role model in that area. Heavens, she could be crowned the patron saint of liars.

"Johnny?" she whispered.

He leapt to his feet, one hand grabbing at his hat to keep it from falling off his head and the other gripping his rib cage.

He winced and groaned.

"Sit down, Johnny." Jenn took his elbow and guided him back to his seat. "I'm sorry," she said. "I didn't mean to startle you."

"You didn't startle me."

"No?" she asked, grinning at him.

He looked stunned for a moment before giving her a cautious smile in return. "Well, maybe just a little bit. I guess I must have dozed off."

"Long night?" she guessed.

"Mmm," he answered pensively.

"For me, too," she admitted.

"Yeah?"

"Yeah," she replied, still smiling at the adorably rumpled cowboy. "Don't you want to know why?"

"I'm not sure I want to hear this," Johnny said, punctuated by another groan. He leaned back on the chair and tipped his hat forward over his eyes, just as he'd been when she first walked up.

"Well, you may not want to hear it, but I have some things to say to you that will not wait."

He sighed heavily. "What did I do now? Whatever it is, I'm really sorry, Jenn."

"Will you stop that already?" she snapped, sounding more irritated than she was feeling. Couldn't the man just be quiet for one minute so she could speak?

"Stop *what* already?"

"Interrupting me!"

"Oh. Sorry."

"And stop saying you're sorry." Now she *was* irritated.

"Okay. Sorry."

She leveled her gaze at him, though his eyes were hidden under the brim of his hat. His lips, however, gave his true feelings away, as they quirked in that endearing way of his.

So he was amused. Teasing her again.

She blushed despite her best efforts. Johnny could get under her skin like no man she'd ever known. He could make her laugh or cry, send her spirit into the heavens or crashing down to earth. It could be frightening, that he had so much power over her, but it wasn't.

Because, she realized without the shadow of a doubt, Johnny would never hurt her, at least not intentionally. What he'd said to her that day at the picnic was true, and she believed it, now that she knew his heart even more than on that day when he'd been a relative stranger to her.

"Given the circumstances," Johnny said, his voice so low and soft, she would hardly have known he was speaking if his lips weren't moving, "I think I should go first."

"You're interrupting again," she reminded him.

"Maybe."

"There is no *maybe* about it."

"But I have some things that need to be said." He tilted his hat up and met her gaze head-on, his midnight-blue eyes serious.

"Be that as it may, you are going to hear me out first," she demanded stubbornly.

"Jenn," he pleaded.

"No. No. Not this time, Johnny."

"What do you mean, *this time?* Seems to me you always get to talk first."

She glared at him, but it was halfhearted. He was right. More often than not, she didn't let him speak first, if at all. Even so, this was one time Jenn *needed* to go first. If she didn't, she might never have the nerve to say what needed to be said.

"I'm going first, and that's all there is to it. You can say anything you please when I'm finished."

"All right."

"All right?" she echoed, having expected at least a token argument from him.

"All right. If there's one thing I've learned about you these past two weeks, Jenn, it's that you're a stubborn woman. No sense fighting with you when I know I'm gonna lose. May as well save my strength."

"Fighting? Johnny, I haven't come to—"

Johnny raised his hands, palms outward, cutting off the flow of her words. "Kidding, Jenn. I'm just pulling your leg."

"You like to get a rise out of me, don't you?" she asked, just a bit surly.

"Yep," he answered, with a cheeky grin. "That I do. Now why don't you sit down here beside me and tell me whatever it is you think I need to hear."

She slid onto the seat next to him, close but not actually touching him. She wanted to reach out to him, but didn't know quite how.

"I just wanted to say I forgive you," she started, deciding the best part of valor was simply to dive in headfirst. "I know you've been keeping secrets from me, but I also know God would not want me holding a grudge against you for your actions, which I'm sure are justified. Even if I don't understand why you hid your true identity from me, I should have realized it didn't matter."

"But it does matter," he argued.

"Johnny, you're interrupting again."

He looked like he was about to say something else, then abruptly clamped his jaw closed.

"The reason it doesn't matter," she continued, "is because I know you. The real you. No matter what your name is. I should have trusted that what I knew in my heart was true about you, rather than go off on a rant the way I did."

"You had every right."

"I had no right. And no excuses. You once told me that you can judge a man by his hat. I've learned a lot in these two weeks, Johnny. I'm not judging you by your hat. I'm judging you by your *heart,* when my own heart has come up wanting."

"Jenn," he whispered in the soft voice that turned her knees to mush. She was glad she was sitting down, or else she might have simply melted into the wooden beams at her feet.

"You are the sweetest, most honorable man I've ever known, Johnny. I was wrong to blame any of this on you. Everything that's happened here is my doing, and I just want you to know I am now taking full responsibility for my actions."

"Jenn," he said again.

"And one more thing."

He reached an arm around her and pulled her close to his side. "And what is that?"

"I wanted to say thank you."

"For?" he drawled lazily, tipping his hat back so his gaze met hers.

"For leaving me that passage in Isaiah. It really spoke to me."

"I'm glad."

"It also reminded me why you're so special."

He groaned and tried to tip his hat back over his eyes, but Jenn wouldn't let him.

"I'm serious. You may not want to hear this, especially now, but I—I care for you very deeply, Johnny. I can be really thickheaded at times, and it's taken me longer than it should have, but I finally realized how happy I am that God brought you into my life."

"Uh—Jenn," Johnny protested, sitting up straight and pulling away from her.

"I'm sorry," she apologized immediately. "I said the wrong thing. Count on me to be candid."

Johnny shook his head, but she waved him off and didn't let him continue.

"I know it's probably too little too late, but I wanted you to know the truth—the whole truth—before you left here forever."

Johnny pulled at the collar of his forest-green Western shirt and shifted again. This time Jenn saw what she'd missed before—Johnny's saddlebags, which had been half-hidden by his boots.

"You're leaving now," she croaked, her voice suddenly giving out.

Johnny pulled his hat off and jammed his fingers through his hair. "That's what I was trying to tell you. After everything that's happened, I thought it would be best if I took off earlier than planned."

"But you can't," Jenn pleaded.

Johnny hadn't expected Jenn's admissions, the way she forgave him even before she knew why he'd deceived her.

He should have seen this coming, he realized belatedly. From the first day they'd met, Jenn had always owned up to her own responsibilities, admitting her own part in whatever she perceived as a problem.

"I've already called for a town car," he explained softly. "It should be here anytime now."

Jenn clasped her hands in her lap and looked away.

"What is it?" he asked. She looked so sad, so distant, that he wanted to reach out to her and wrap her in his arms. But if he did that, he knew he'd never be able to let her go, so he remained still.

It was a long time before Jenn spoke. When she did, she slipped her hand into Johnny's and met his gaze squarely. "I don't want you to go," she said in a voice barely above a whisper.

Whatever Johnny had expected, it wasn't that. Sure, she'd just openly admitted to having feelings for him, something that made his heart soar. But he still thought he should leave.

Even if Jenn didn't realize it right now, his leaving would be best for everyone involved. He'd already caused Jenn more pain than he ever would have wished. All he wanted to do was protect her and care for her.

Love her.

All the more reason he ought to walk away right now, before things got even more complicated. Before he managed to hurt the woman he loved even more.

"I think it would be best," he said at last.

She stood and glared down at him, her hands planted firmly on her hips. "Best for whom?" she bit out.

He stood and faced her, ignoring the pain in his rib cage. "For you, I think," he replied, trying to keep the emotion he was feeling from showing in his voice, a task at which he was not entirely successful.

"Why don't you let me be the judge of that?" she said, leaning over to pick up his saddlebags, which she promptly shoved at his chest.

He winced. "Look, Jenn, I thought a lot about this last night, which is why I didn't get any sleep, as you so adroitly pointed out. I really think it would be best for me to leave today. Now."

"Well, I don't," she snapped back. "And neither does my family. Did you think about them when you made this rash decision?"

"Of course I thought about your family," he replied, testily. "Jenn, these have been the happiest two weeks of my life. I've never spent time with a real family before, and I can't tell you what a blessing it's been to me. What a blessing *you've* been to me."

"Then stay."

"I can't. I just can't." How could he try to explain to her the anguish in his heart? How could he make her understand that he just had to walk away now—before he couldn't walk away at all?

"Yes, you can. And you will. For me, Johnny. If you care for me at all, like you told me you did, then you will be man enough to stick around and see it through to the end."

"I just don't want to hurt you anymore," he said softly, looking away from her piercing gaze.

"Johnny Barnes, you could never hurt me. You told me that yourself, the day of the picnic."

"But I have, don't you see?"

"What I see is a dumb, obstinate cowboy who doesn't know when to say give. You aren't going to wrestle this calf to the ground, Johnny, so you may as well give up and accept it."

He chuckled lowly. She was quite a woman, his Jenn. Bullheaded as the day was long.

And he loved her for it.

Gazing straight into her wide blue eyes, he dangled the saddlebags in front of her and then dropped them at her feet.

"That's better," she said with the brightest smile he'd ever seen from her lips. Her entire face lit up when she smiled that way. If she was pretty before, she was knock-down, drag-out beautiful right this second.

It was all he could do not to pull her into his arms and kiss the daylights out of her. He clenched his fists against the urge, groaning with the effort.

She was by his side in a second, supporting him with her arms around his waist. "What is it, your ribs? Sit down, Johnny."

He closed his eyes. Her scent, all flowers and beautiful woman, wafted around him until he was dizzy. His resistance was weakening by the second, and he knew it. "If you stay where you're at," he warned her with a low growl, "I'm going to kiss you."

She threw back her head and laughed. "Is that supposed to be a threat—or a warning?"

"It's a warning," he rumbled low in his throat. "I suggest you take it to heart."

"Make no mistake," she said, shifting her arms so she was face-to-face with him. "I intend to."

It was as if time slowed. Johnny forgot to breathe when Jenn reached up and stroked his jaw with her long, soft fingers. She reached around to the back of his neck, drawing his head down toward hers.

He couldn't fight her. He didn't even want to. His eyes drifted closed as their lips met. Her kiss was soft and innocent, like the woman herself.

He was lost and he knew it. Without a care for his rib cage, which he couldn't feel anyway, beneath the pounding of his heart, he wrapped his arms around her and drew her closer, putting all the emotions of the past few days into a long and thorough kiss.

At long last he pulled away, tucking Jenn's head into his chest, where they stood for the longest time, unmoving. She clung to him as much as he was clinging to her, and he was glad for that, thinking they might both fall over if they were to be separated.

The sound of a car driving up the dirt road to the

ranch house pulled Johnny out of his reverie. The town car he'd called for was here to pick him up.

"Jenn," he said hoarsely.

"Mmm?"

"My town car is here."

"Oh." She sounded confused. Flustered. "I forgot about the car."

"So did I," he said with a chuckle. He'd forgotten about everything but Jenn and the myriad of feelings still coursing through him.

"What are you going to do?" Her voice was as rough as his, an observation which made him smile all the wider. The poor woman looked genuinely distressed, and for some reason, that made his chest well up with so much emotion he thought he might burst.

He chucked her under the chin. "No worries, darlin'. Just give me a second."

Jenn's breath caught in her throat as she watched Johnny approach the car and speak with the driver. He'd left his saddlebags at her feet.

She hoped it meant what she thought it meant. After the special moment they'd just shared, she couldn't see how he could possibly leave.

They had a lot to talk about.

After a minute, Johnny stood to his full height and tapped his hand a couple times on the hood of the car. The car pulled away and Johnny turned and grinned at her.

"I paid him for his time," he explained, as he approached her, "and sent him on his merry way—without me tagging along."

Jenn smiled back. She still couldn't breathe, never mind speak, around the lump of emotion in her throat.

"So then, I'm all yours for the next couple of days. If I have my way, we'll be spending every second together. There's so much I don't know about you. So much more I want to learn."

"I want that, too," Jenn said, finally regaining the use of her voice. "Johnny, that must have cost you a fortune, sending the car away."

Johnny laughed and winked at her. "Darlin', don't worry about it. I *have* a fortune. And I'd gladly spend a hundred times the amount I gave that driver, if it meant I got to spend the rest of the week with you."

"Will you go back to the range with Scotty?" she asked, not liking the feeling she got at thinking of Johnny going anywhere away from her.

"Yep," he answered without hesitation. "I signed on for the summer, and I'm giving them the summer, no matter how hard it might be for me to fulfill my obligations to the ranch."

Jenn nodded slowly. "I understand, even if I don't like it very much. And I respect your decision to honor your contract."

"Thank you," he said in that soft, low voice of his. "It looks like we'll be doing just what you said we were doing at that family dinner of yours—e-mailing each other and making phone calls whenever my cell phone has service."

"This is going to be hard, isn't it?"

"Maybe the hardest trial I've ever had to endure," Johnny said, sincerely. He stroked a hand down her cheek. "But we can do this, you and I. And I have the feeling I may be spending an awful lot of time in Denver, once I get back to my regular job."

"You live in New York. That's an awful long way from Denver."

"Not for a jet-setter like me," he teased. "I spend half my time on an airplane, as it is. I'll just make sure the airplane in question is headed for Denver."

Warmth filled Jenn at Johnny's words. He was willing to go to any lengths to be with her. He genuinely cherished her, something that she'd never before felt from a man.

And this wasn't just any man. This was Johnny Barnes. Or more precisely, Jonathan Barnes-Whitcomb. No matter what his name was, he was hers.

Impulsively, she threw her arms around Johnny and hugged him tight, making him wince and laugh simultaneously.

He would always be Johnny Barnes, the cowboy, to her. She couldn't even picture him in a business suit, with his wild curls tamed and slicked back.

It would be interesting, getting to know that side of him, the teenage prodigy who'd contributed so much to society with his genius.

But for now, she was simply going to enjoy the sweet, humble cowboy in her arms. She tilted her head up to look into his face. His midnight-blue eyes were twinkling, and his lips turned up in amusement.

"Darlin', if you keep looking at me like that, I'm going to have to kiss you again."

"I was hoping you'd say that."

Johnny obliged her readily, tilting his head down to kiss her once again. She loved the paradoxical combination of strength and tenderness in his touch.

"Well, well, if that don't beat all," Auntie Myra said loudly, from behind Jenn's left shoulder.

Jenn and Johnny broke apart instantly, both of them looking as guilty as kids with their hands stuck in the cookie jar.

"Oh, don't stop on my account," Auntie Myra said, with a cackling laugh. "Don't mind me at all."

"Ahem." Jenn cleared her throat so she could speak, or at least attempt to speak. "Did you want something?"

Johnny slipped an arm around Jenn's waist and laughed wholeheartedly. "Looks like you caught us again, Auntie Myra."

"I'm sure I did," Auntie Myra replied, with a wink at Jenn that made the younger woman blush in mortification.

"Actually, I was sent to find you both for luncheon. Granny has outdone herself, as usual. There's enough food on the dining table to feed a whole next generation of Washingtons—or whatever their last name might happen to be."

Auntie Myra laughed at her own joke, and Jenn found, if it were possible, that she was blushing even more than before.

A whole new generation...

Epilogue

December

Jenn had a backlog of paperwork to be done and was preparing for yet another late night, when the office secretary buzzed her desk.

"Ms. Washington, Mr. Whitcomb is here to see you."

Johnny.

This was a surprise. It had been two weeks since she'd seen him, and hadn't expected him again until next week, when they planned to spend Christmas Eve together, going to the midnight church service and exchanging presents afterward.

She'd even bought a tree, albeit a predecorated, artificial pine, for her apartment for the occasion. Never before had she had a Christmas tree in her home. Never before had she felt like celebrating the way she did this year, with her dear Johnny.

She would never get used to seeing him in Armani, his gorgeous curly hair gelled and slicked back. He cut a fine picture, to be sure; but somehow, Jenn felt something was always missing from the picture.

Probably a cowboy hat and boots, she thought with a smile.

To think, she was in love with a cowboy.

"Hey there, darlin'," Johnny drawled from the doorway.

Jenn looked up from her paperwork to find Johnny casually leaning his broad shoulder against the door frame, that amused quirk on his lips and a bouquet of roses thrust forward in one hand.

"Love, Me," he said with a chuckle.

"Johnny," she exclaimed, rising from her chair and launching herself full-force into his arms. "I didn't expect you until Christmas Eve."

"Maybe Santa's coming early this year," he said, throwing his head back for a hearty laugh. "Watch it, love, you're squishing the roses."

Jenn didn't care about the flowers. All she wanted was to be in Johnny's arms, and to stay there.

It was only then, in his arms, that she realized her cheek was nuzzling flannel, not fine silk. Glancing at the man she held so dear, she was pleased to find him in jeans and cowboy boots, his black Diamond Jim hat in one hand.

"I like you better this way," she whispered, hugging him tightly.

"I like me better this way, too," he said, framing her face with one hand for a most welcome kiss. "Now, then, I've come to rescue you from that huge pile of paperwork I see on your desk. You were planning to work late again, weren't you?"

He made the idea sound so awful, Jenn tried to shrug

it off. "It has to be done," she said, just a tad defensively. "I always feel like I'm behind."

"Darlin', it's Friday night. This is *definitely not* how you should be spending your Friday nights."

"No?" she teased lightly. "You have a better idea in mind?"

"Actually, I do."

"And that would be...?"

"Reservations. At the finest, most exclusive dining facility in the whole Denver metropolitan area."

"Which restaurant?" she asked.

"It's a surprise. Come on, get your coat. We're going to swing by your house so you can change into something more comfortable—say jeans and a Western shirt?"

"I'm quite comfortable in my work clothes," she informed him, brushing down her wool skirt. "Besides, how is it that we can be going to an exclusive restaurant dressed in jeans?"

"Now *that* is for me to know and you to find out. Trust me on this one, please, Jenn?"

How could she resist, when he was asking so nicely?

In half an hour, Johnny had her back to her apartment, her lovely red roses carefully arranged in the vase she had purchased for the family reunion.

It was fitting, as if her life had come full circle. Her world was beginning to make sense to her. Things were falling into place at last.

She hoped.

Jenn quickly changed into blue jeans and an emerald-colored Western shirt with pearl snaps. She even had cowboy boots now, the real kind, meant for riding horses, for when she next made a trip to the ranch.

"You look fantastic," Johnny said, as she slipped into the back of the limousine he'd rented.

"Thanks, I think," she replied, making a face at him. "How did I get hooked up with a cowboy, anyway?"

He chuckled. "That, darlin', is a long story, and you'd never believe a word of it. Anyway, we'd better hurry now, or we'll lose our reservation."

"Are you going to tell me where we're going?" she asked again.

He smiled. "Chez Barnes," he said. "I finally broke down and bought a condo here."

"That's wonderful!" she exclaimed, and then stopped short and shot him a pointed look. "Don't tell me you cooked a meal."

"Me? I don't think so—not unless you want baked beans out of a can, cooked over an open fire."

Jenn scrunched up her nose. "So we're having takeout, then?" It still sounded romantic, and Johnny had obviously gone to a lot of trouble for her.

"Something like that," he said wryly.

When they got to his condo, he stopped in front of the door, his key in his hand. "This is it," he said with a grand sweep of his arm. "Chez Barnes. And you are a most welcome guest here."

He swept open the door and Jenn peered into the dark room, unable to see any more than the shadows of the sparse furniture there.

Jenn had expected something bigger, more elegant, somehow. Johnny had the money, after all. But his condo was small and practical.

Humble, like her cowboy.

Johnny ushered her in the door and to the middle of the room, not pausing to turn on any lights.

"Very romantic, Johnny, but don't you think we need at least a few candles, or a fire in the fireplace, or something? I can't see a thing."

Suddenly the whole room lit up.

"Surprise!" yelled a cacophony of voices from around the room.

Jenn screamed—literally screamed—in surprise.

Surprise didn't even begin to cover it. All her family members were merging on her—every single one of them, even Scotty.

"A little birdie told me it was your birthday," Johnny whispered into her ear from behind her, his breath soft on the nape of her neck. "Surely you haven't forgotten your own birthday."

She turned and rested her palms against the wide expanse of his chest. "That little birdie should have kept her mouth shut," she grumbled good-naturedly. Actually, she was thrilled to see her family again. She'd been missing them.

"*His* mouth, actually," Johnny replied with a chuckle.

Jenn sent a friendly glare in her brother's direction, but Scotty just tipped his cavalry hat at her and grinned from ear to ear.

"Is this a conspiracy?" she asked the room at large, planting her fists on her hips for emphasis.

"Count on it, darlin'," Johnny replied, wrapping his arm around her shoulder. "We can't have you working late on your birthday, now can we? Ask yourself, what would your family think of me if I didn't make a big celebration for you?"

Tears welled in Jenn's eyes. No one had ever made a birthday celebration for her, not since she'd left home. She'd always been alone on her birthday, and had planned to be alone yet again this year.

Johnny had changed all that. And now her family, too. Her heart welled with gratitude and love, until she thought she might burst from feeling.

"Aw, don't cry, darlin'," Johnny crooned. "I hate it when women cry. It breaks me all up inside."

"Me, too," Jenn said with a half-chuckle, half-hiccup as she dabbed at the tears in her eyes. "I never cry. I don't know what's wrong with me."

"I do," crowed Auntie Myra. "Love. That's what it is, sweetheart. Love."

"Cut it out, Myra," Granny demanded. "You're embarrassing the poor girl."

Granddad grunted his concurrence with the statement Granny had made.

"You know your Auntie Myra is just poking fun at you," Jenn's father said, as Johnny drew her farther into the room, which she now saw had been decorated with purple and gold balloons and streamers.

Her favorite colors.

How had Johnny known? He'd obviously been in touch with her family.

"Do you like your cake?" Johnny asked, every bit as expectant as a small boy, his expression clearly eager for her answer.

Jenn gazed at the homemade masterpiece, two layers smothered in chocolate buttercream frosting. A ballerina music box had been carefully placed in the middle, in between the words *Happy Birthday, Jenn.*

Johnny leaned around her and wound up the music box. The soft, tinny melody of "Lorelei" drifted across the room, but in Jenn's mind, it was the Elvis Presley lyrics she was hearing, a love song.

"Do you like it?" Johnny asked in that rich, soft-spoken voice Jenn so loved.

"I love it."

I love you.

She didn't say the words aloud, but she was certain they were in her eyes for all the world to see.

"I made it," Johnny said excitedly.

"You did *what?* I don't believe you," Jenn exclaimed, jabbing Johnny's arm. "You don't cook any more than I do."

"Well, I made this cake," he said with a mock-defensive posture.

Granny chuckled. "With a little help from his family, that is."

"Oh," Jenn said, drawing out the word. "Now I get it. You got to lick the frosting out of the bowl, right, Johnny?"

"He baked the cake," Scotty said with a laugh. "I watched him. If you look real close, you can see it's kind of lopsided."

"Hey," said Johnny, "thanks for pointing that out to her, sport. I was hoping she wouldn't notice."

"You really made a cake for me," Jenn said, wonder lining her voice as she believed him at last.

"I did. And it *is* a little lopsided. But it's the thought that counts, right?"

"Most definitely," she assured him. "And I'm sure it will taste just wonderful."

"Let's get this party started, then," Granny announced without preamble. "Someone light the candles."

Jenn's mother lit the two candles—the number Two on one side of the cake and the number Seven on the other.

"Time to cowboy-up and make a wish, darlin'," Johnny said softly, guiding her to the front of the cake, with his hands on her waist. "Make it a good one."

Jenn closed her eyes for a moment, enjoying the peace and joy of the moment. Then she made her wish, a simple prayer, really, that she might find many more of these special times with her family.

And with Johnny.

She opened her eyes and blew out the candles. Everyone hooted and applauded.

"Let's rodeo!" Scotty exclaimed with a hearty laugh.

"Speaking of rodeo," Johnny said to Jenn, but loud enough for everyone in the room to hear, "I think it's about time I cowboy-up, as well."

With that, he dropped to one knee in front of Jenn and held out a small velvet jewelry case. "How 'bout it, darlin'? Will you marry me?"

Jenn stared down at him for a moment, not believing her own eyes. At length, she shook the feeling and smiled as she reached for Johnny's hand to pull him to his feet.

"The cowboy or the businessman?" she quipped.

Johnny chuckled and shrugged. "I'm afraid you'll have to take the whole lot."

"I see." She paused thoughtfully. "That's quite a challenge. However," she said, staring deeply into his brilliant midnight-blue eyes, "I do believe I'm up to it. I will marry you, Johnny Barnes and Jonathan Whitcomb."

Her family, which Jenn had temporarily forgotten were even in the room, broke into applause, hoots and cheers.

"Well, whatever my last name will be," she said, with a soft, happy smile, "I think there might be a few more little Whatever-Their-Last-Name-Is feet pattering around in future family reunions. Hopefully, at least one with his father's gorgeous black curls."

Johnny wrapped his arms around her shoulders and squeezed her close. "I can't vouch for hair color," he said, close to her ear, "but as for little ones? Nothing would make me happier."

"Or me," Auntie Myra chimed in.

"Or me!" added Granny. "And it's about time, too, if you ask me."

For once, Jenn agreed with her family.

* * * * *

Dear Reader,

This book is a direct result of one of my favorite hobbies. I was researching and watching the complete filmography of my favorite television actor, Dale Midkiff, whom you might know from his role as Clark Davis in the *Love Comes Softly* movies.

I ran across a television series from the late nineties called *The Magnificent Seven*. This wonderful series was a take-off on the old movie. These seven delightful gunslingers renewed my interest in writing a dashing cowboy hero, and from that came *A Wedding in Wyoming*.

I hope you have as good a time reading about my charming cowboy as I enjoyed writing about him.

I love to hear from my readers. I hope to have my own Web page up and running soon. In the meantime, you can contact me by e-mail at DEBWRTR@aol.com, or on my MySpace or Facebook pages. I look forward to hearing from you!

In Christ's Love,

Deb Kastner

QUESTIONS FOR DISCUSSION

1. Jenn struggles with circumstances beyond her control. What circumstances in your life feel beyond your control? Discuss how you handle these situations. How can you trust God when things go wrong?

2. Jenn had been physically abused in her youth. Have you suffered from physical abuse, or do you know someone in this situation? How can you minister to those who have suffered physical abuse? Can you ever move on, or do you just learn to live with it?

3. In the book, Jenn wants to control everything. It was only when she realizes she is *not* in control that she can trust God and move on with her life. In what practical ways can you "hand over the reins" to God when it seems life is moving beyond your control?

4. To which character in *A Wedding in Wyoming* do you most relate? Why?

5. What do you consider the themes of *A Wedding in Wyoming?* How do they relate to your life?

6. Jenn has issues with lying. Is it ever right to lie? What about little white lies? How can you resolve to tell the truth in your own life?

7. During the course of the book, Johnny wears a couple of different "coats," or identities. All of us

wear a number of "coats," such as wife, mother, daughter, career woman, etc. What "coats" do you wear? How do you balance them?

8. Jenn's extended family was a very important part of her life, and Johnny didn't have a family. What kind of role does your extended family play in your life? Who are the spiritual patriarchs/matriarchs in your family?

9. Some people don't come from a Christian background when they come to faith in Christ. Specifically, in what ways can they start, where they are at, to develop their own Christian legacy?

10. Jenn struggles with her own fear—fear of the past repeating itself and fear in trusting God with her life and her future. Share a fear you have in your own life, and how you can give that fear to God and find peace.

11. In the book, Johnny takes a sabbatical from his "real" life and in the process grows closer to God. Do you need to distance yourself from anything or anyone in order to renew your strength and your focus on God?

12. Jenn forgives Johnny unconditionally, without waiting to hear his explanation for his actions. Why do you think she does this? Read Matthew 6:12, which is part of The Lord's Prayer, and discuss the implications in your own life.

13. Because of her past, Jenn was angry with God. Have you ever been angry with God? How did God work in your life to resolve that situation?

14. Johnny uses bible verses to minister to Jenn, when his own words are not enough. We can't use the scriptures to speak to others unless we know them ourselves. In what ways do you place the word of God in your heart? How can you do better?

15. Has there ever been a situation where you used the bible to minister to another person? What was the result?

Here is an exciting sneak preview of
TWIN TARGETS by Marta Perry,
the first book in the new 6-book
Love Inspired Suspense series
PROTECTING THE WITNESSES,
available beginning January 2010.

Deputy U.S. Marshal Micah McGraw forced down the sick feeling in his gut. A law enforcement professional couldn't get emotional about crime victims. He could imagine his police chief father saying the words. Or his FBI agent big brother. They wouldn't let emotion interfere with doing the job.

"Pity." The local police chief grunted.

Natural enough. The chief hadn't known Ruby Maxwell, aka Ruby Summers. He hadn't been the agent charged with relocating her to this supposedly safe environment in a small village in Montana. He didn't have to feel responsible for her death.

"This looks like a professional hit," Chief Burrows said.

"Yeah."

He knew only too well what was in the man's mind. What would a professional hit man be doing in the remote reaches of western Montana? Why would anyone want to kill this seemingly inoffensive waitress?

And most of all, what did the U.S. Marshals Service have to do with it?

All good questions. Unfortunately he couldn't answer any of them. Secrecy was the crucial element that made the Federal Witness Protection Service so successful. Breach that, and everything that had been gained in the battle against organized crime would be lost.

His cell buzzed and he turned away to answer it. "McGraw."

"You wanted the address for the woman's next of kin?" asked one of his investigators.

"Right." Ruby had a twin sister, he knew. She'd have to be notified. Since she lived back east, at least he wouldn't be the one to do that.

"Jade Summers. Librarian. Current address is 45 Rock Lane, White Rock, Montana."

For an instant Micah froze. "Are you sure of that?"

"'Course I'm sure."

After he hung up, Micah turned to stare once more at the empty shell that had been Ruby Summers. She'd made mistakes in her life, plenty of them, but she'd done the right thing in the end when she'd testified against the mob. She hadn't deserved to end up lifeless on a cold concrete floor.

As for her sister…

What exactly was an easterner like Jade Summers doing in a small town in Montana? If there was an innocent reason, he couldn't think of it.

Ruby must have tipped her off to her location. That was the only explanation, and the deed violated one of the major principles of witness protection.

Ruby had known the rules. Immediate family could

be relocated with her. If they chose not to, no contact was permitted—ever.

Ruby's twin had moved to Montana. White Rock was probably forty miles or so east of Billings. Not exactly around the corner from her sister.

But the fact that she was in Montana had to mean that they'd been in contact. And that contact just might have led to Ruby's death.

He glanced at his watch. Once his team arrived, he'd get back on the road toward Billings and beyond, to White Rock. To find Jade Summers and get some answers.

* * * * *

Will Micah get to Jade in time to
save her from a similar fate?
Find out in TWIN TARGETS,
available January 2010
from Love Inspired Suspense.

Cheyenne Rhodes has come to Redemption, Oklahoma, to start anew, not to make new friends. But single dad Trace Bowman isn't about to let her hide her heart away. He just needs to convince Cheyenne that Redemption is more than a place to hide—it's also a way to be found....

Look for

Finding Her Way Home

by

Linda Goodnight

REDEMPTION
RIVER

*Available January
wherever books are sold.*

www.SteepleHill.com

Steeple
Hill®
LI87571

LARGER-PRINT BOOKS!

GET 2 FREE
LARGER-PRINT NOVELS
PLUS 2 FREE
MYSTERY GIFTS

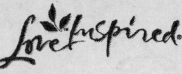

Larger-print novels are now available...

YES! Please send me 2 FREE LARGER-PRINT Love Inspired® novels and my 2 FREE mystery gifts (gifts are worth about $10). After receiving them, if I don't wish to receive any more books, I can return the shipping statement marked "cancel". If I don't cancel, I will receive 4 brand-new novels every month and be billed just $4.49 per book in the U.S. or $4.99 per book in Canada. That's a savings of over 30% off the cover price. It's quite a bargain! Shipping and handling is just 50¢ per book.* I understand that accepting the 2 free books and gifts places me under no obligation to buy anything. I can always return a shipment and cancel at any time. Even if I never buy another book, the two free books and gifts are mine to keep forever.

121 IDN EYLZ 321 IDN EYME

Name _____ (PLEASE PRINT) _____

Address _____ Apt. # _____

City _____ State/Prov. _____ Zip/Postal Code _____

Signature (if under 18, a parent or guardian must sign)

Mail to Steeple Hill Reader Service:

IN U.S.A.: P.O. Box 1867, Buffalo, NY 14240-1867
IN CANADA: P.O. Box 609, Fort Erie, Ontario L2A 5X3

**Are you a current subscriber of Love Inspired books
and want to receive the larger-print edition?
Call 1-800-873-8635 or visit www.morefreebooks.com.**

* Terms and prices subject to change without notice. Prices do not include applicable taxes. Sales tax applicable in N.Y. Canadian residents will be charged applicable provincial taxes and GST. Offer not valid in Quebec. This offer is limited to one order per household. All orders subject to approval. Credit or debit balances in a customer's account(s) may be offset by any other outstanding balance owed by or to the customer. Please allow 4 to 6 weeks for delivery. Offer available while quantities last.

> **Your Privacy:** Steeple Hill Books is committed to protecting your privacy. Our Privacy Policy is available online at www.SteepleHill.com or upon request from the Reader Service. From time to time we make our lists of customers available to reputable third parties who may have a product or service of interest to you. ☐
> If you would prefer we not share your name and address, please check here.

LILP09

TITLES AVAILABLE NEXT MONTH
Available December 29, 2009

LICNMBPA1209